The Back Streets o the Claw

The BACK STREETS *o the* CLAW

Philip Robinson

SECOND EDITION

ULSTER-SCOTS ACADEMY PRESS

First Published by Ullans Press, 2000

Second edition by the Ulster-Scots Academy Press, 2021

This novel is a sequel to:

Wake the Tribe o Dan (Second edition, 2020)

Also by the same author:

Esther, Quaen o tha Ulidian Pechts (1997)
Fergus an tha Stane o Destinie (1999)
The Man Frae the Ministry (2005)
Alang tha Shore (2006)
The Old Orange Tree (2009)
Oul Licht, New Licht (2009)

For Amy, Beth and Fergus

ISBN 978-1-9163758-3-3

Ephie's base bairntime, trail-pike brood,
Were arm'd as weel as tribes that stood;
Yet on the battle ilka cauf,
Turn'd his backside, an' scamper'd aff.
> Psalm 78, v. 9.
> (James Orr, Ballycarry, 1804)

Lines paraphrased from Psalm 78 into Ulster-Scots after the Battle of Antrim, 1798, when the insurgent "Army of Ulster," including the poet Orr, scattered from their mustering camp at nearby Donegore Hill.

The children of Ephraim, being armed, and carrying bows,
turned back in the day of battle.
They kept not the covenant of God, and refused to walk in his
law.

(King James' Bible, 1611)

CONTENTS

Chapter 1

A Good Match

Ten thousand chimneys in wee rows, running this road and that. Every reeking lum-pot was proof – a living, breathing proof – of warm hearts and warm hearths below.

That was the Claw and the neighbouring streets, like a mighty redbrick regiment ranked the length of the Blackfort Road. These uniform, red house-fronts had stood, unblinking, for a hundred years of Empire. Walking down them was as if you were inspecting ranks of private lives – or trespassing behind enemy lines, if you came from the wrong part of Bigganreek.

From afar, like an army on an opposite hill, it seemed as if this multitude had just one purpose in mind. But such an army was easier to raise than to stand down. The Heidyins of Church, State and Industry had precious little use for such a muster nowadays, no matter what they said in public. And they had long forgotten what the chief end of it all was, in the first place. It was a problem area right enough.

Up close, the uniformity broke down. Behind each and every door a different world existed. Thran independence of thought was the only birthright, and not one family of a single mind on any subject. The men, women and childer of the Claw had a reputation for being single-minded. If you were to call them "tight-knit" you would be missing the point.

They came from all arts and parts of the countryside, or at least their forebears had, gathering here three or four generations back. Barely a century separated most of them from their rural roots, but there was no nostalgia for anything like that. Family trees were left to rot, and with that went the folk memory of home farms, townlands and kinship connections.

Ernie Gamble and John M'Clean senior had spent all their married lives at opposite ends of the Claw, living twenty streets apart. For the same length of time they had worked in different "shops" in the shipyard. It was hardly surprising that their lives had never crossed, since there were thousands of other folk answering to the same history.

Ernie didn't know about his great-grandfather leaving Drumcrun for a horse-handling job in Bigganreek nearly a hundred years ago. Well, he had heard his father mention a stabling yard that some old boy connected to them used to work in, but that was all. John M'Clean didn't know that his wife's grandmother came from Drumcrun Upper at the same time. Indeed, his wife Bessie neither knew nor cared about such things herself. She might have been interested if she'd been told that these two bygone flitters had known each other, in the Biblical sense.

They met only once, Ernie and John, if it could be called a meeting. The last luxury liner to be built in the Yard was being launched. Ernie was retiring after 40 years and John M'Clean was going on short time again, with the completion of the order.

"They expect us to cheer," John M'Clean said to the man beside him.

"Well, I've somethin' to cheer about," Ernie Gamble answered without taking his eyes off the enormous steel hulk that ground its way down into the water, jerking steel wires and dragging thundering, rumbling chains behind it. "That's my last ship, an' that's me done workin' for yer man."

"Ye givin' up work, then, retirin', like?"

"Ay," Ernie said, glancing proudly round at him.

"Ye'll be your own boss from now," John said, taking his pipe out of his mouth to smile.

"Ye haven't met the wife, then?" Ernie said, and they both laughed and turned back to the spectacle.

In a few years John M'Clean junior would be courting Ernie's daughter. But at that point, neither past nor future meeting of the two families' paths meant anything.

At home and at work, Ernie was known as a thinker. It was surprising, then, that he thought so little of his roots.

"What's thon spirals mean on them oul gravestones?" This was the sort of question that got Ernie going. That particular starter for ten was in the Friesian Bull, on the first Saturday after his retirement.

"It's the mystery o' life."

After a pause, the full explanation was given. "Ye see, ye have a circle at the outside, that's like infinity, no start an' no endin'. And ye go roun' an' roun' the spiral till ye come to a dot in the middle. That's the same. Whatever road ye go, ye end up at infinity."

Like all Ernie's explanations, it wasn't.

"Ay?" was the only possible response.

Maybe Ernie did understand the mystery of life. He seemed to be just as likely a candidate as any, for he wasn't trying to sell you religion. On such occasions, Ernie was a master at keeping the curious guessing.

"Ye have two parents, don't ye? And four grandparents, and eight great grandparents, and so on and so on? Well if ye keep goin' back far enough, ye'll find ye've come down from an infinite number o' ancestors. Simple mathematics. Right?"

Another pause.

"But it starts the other way roun' from Adam an' Eve. And they have two weans and four grandweans, and eight greatgrandchilder, and so on, till ye end up wi' an infinite number o' childern. If we keep on goin'. So. It's the mystery o' life. No matter what way ye go, back or forwards, ye come to infinity."

But even to somebody who was a one-off like Ernie, folksy origins from generations back were of no possible interest. In this respect at least, he was exactly like the rest of the Claw. Their speech had been stripped, deliberately and willingly, of its distinctive Ulster-Scots. And as proud working men, townies to the core, they had also set their face against backward country ways. Yet for all that, they were who they were. And they knew they all had come from the same tribal vortex, "for a' that."

Perhaps, on the surface, the dialogue of their outward life was no longer recognisably Ulster-Scots. But the connecting narrative of their very existence was still underwritten with the signature of that hill-billie nation.

Jack wasnae a wakerife sort o a body. In fact he was aye the last in the M'Clean household to rise. But this Monday morning was cold and he hadnae slept well. Doon the stairs he came, to the sicht o his mother's hefty back obscuring the kitchen range. The sickish feeling he had in the pit o his stomach was mair nor likely nerves, he thocht. This shouldnae happen wae a carefree lad that was just left school a wheen o months. Nae mair "eckers" frae school, and he had his ain wage packet frae Wetheral's canning factory. But the new spirit o freedom had proved short-lived.

"Ye're not goin' out thon door wi'out a dacent breakfast

in ye, so ye're not."

His mother turned on him as she whanged the frying pan doon on the stove. What you saw was twice what you got wae her. Jack's father came doon the stairs dressed for work too. He paused near the bottom and jooked under ceiling height, keeking ower the rail into the kitchen-parlour.

"Ye not away yet, Jack?"

"Ay, I'm aff now da," Jack answered as he put his coat on and squeezed oot the front door past his father at the foot o the stairs.

"In the Name o' Dear," Mrs M'Clean said as soon as the door was pulled shut, "give thon wee fella a shout. He's away up the street wi'out his piece." She pushed a greaseproof-paper parcel o veda sandwiches into her husband's chest.

John M'Clean, senior, lifted his empty pipe and took a wee Scotch draw frae it afore putting it back on the mantelpiece, carefully, and as slow as he dared. Then he did what he was bid. When he came back in, Mrs M'Clean was waiting in the door through to the working kitchen, ready to continue.

"What's up wi' our Jack this weather?" she demanded.

"Ach what's wrong wi' ye now?" John said, mair in defence o himsel than his son.

"There's nathin' wrong wi' me. See him but."

"Ay?"

"He comes down them stairs an' sez he cud'n face his fry. Then he sez, 'have ye any grapefruit?' I ast ye – grapefruit!"

"An' what's wrong wi' that then?" John said. "He's a workin' man now. Sure he can ate what he wants."

Mrs M'Clean gien her man a soor look that would hae turned an orange into a grapefruit.

"It's thon wee huzzy from the low en' o' the Claw he's startit up wi'. Dear knows what other company he's keepin'." She paused briefly to eye her husband. "A fat lot you care," she added, when she saw a bit mair prodding was necessary to get a response.

"There's nathin' wrong wi' any o' the Gambles – sure isn't the wee girl one o' our own sort? Ye're just feart o' Jack leavin' home."

"There's no good iver come out o' thon en' o' the Claw yet. Just you mark my words."

John sat down in his ain seat by the range and put his dry pipe back in his mooth as the wife stomped off into the working-kitchen.

"A'll just have some scrambled eggs," he called out, and sat back wae a wee smirk, waiting for the explosion.

The formidable bulk of Mrs M'Clean returned, waving an empty frying pan in her man's face.

"I'll scrammle you, ye oul eejit," she said. The oul eejit was unmoved.

"What are ye for makin' wi' that now?" John said, pointing recklessly at the pan with his pipe. "The beds?"

"Oh ye're a quare geg," she said. "The day you make the beds, never mind eggs, is the day we'll all have a good laugh."

"It's time I was away," John said.

"Ay, away you on an' all, till I get ma head shired o' the both o' yis."

Jack junior looked back doon Champion Street when he got the length o the Blackfort Road. He scanned the red and yellow fronts o the terraced houses. The scrambled egg pattern o bricks on the better side o the street wasnae broke by a single apen door. There was just yin other body in the streets. He spotted the dapper figure o Walter Dibber ahint him, and waited. He wasnae in much o a mood for Walter's company, but there was mair nor good manners involved. After all, Walter was the only yin in Champion Street wae an office job. Or, at least, he was the only one who went to work in a shirt and tie, for he wrocht in a jeweller's shop doon near the city centre. Walter's twa shiney shune, his licht overcoat and his wee broon trilby hat all set him a cut abane the rest. He had gien Jack a good reference for his job in Ulidican – or Wetheral's as maist folk cried it – and for years had helped Jack wae music lessons on the trombone.

"How's about ye Walter?"

"Mornin' Jack – family all well?"

"Yea, keepin' bravely thanks."

"And your young lady?"

"Grand too, thanks."

Mention o Lily Gamble set Jack's stomach turning again. No that there was onie problems between them. They were still in the early throes o courtship, but were easy eneuch in each other's company. It was just something Lily had said on Saturday nicht that he kept dwelling on. The words had gone round his heid even mair last nicht than in the early hours o Sunday morning: "Our Billy scz the boss wants to see you on Monday." "What for?" Jack had answered, anxious-like. "No idea, so A haven't," Lily replied. "Ye haven't been skivin' off have ye?" "Wise up, sure ye know A haven't," Jack answered, a taste ower snappy. For some unknown reason, Lily hated being told to "wise up." "There's no need to ate the bake aff me," Lily said, hurt. "I'm sorry," Jack had said, giving her waist a squeeze wae baith hands. "It's just … has Billy or you ever been sent for?"

He hadnae wrocht at the food factory as lang as Lily or her brother. In fact, the mair he was going oot wae Lily for even less time than he had been in work, he felt mair secure in their relationship than he did in his job. But he didnae want to lose either.

On their first few dates Jack had all the nervous anticipation he could thole. Would she stand him up or no? When she did turn up a bit late, he still didnae relax tae he saw her smile. "A born worry" she called him, whiles, and maybe she was richt.

Yin reason Jack noo felt sure about their going steady state was the standing arrangement they had for ganging in to work thegither every morning. There was nae need for either of them to worry about their routine o meeting up on the Blackfort Road. You never played hard to get wae your employer.

Walter only walked a wee bit of the way wae Jack. As soon as they reached the trolley-bus stop on the Blackfort Road, Walter stopped to join the queue.

"See ye Walter," Jack said as he left him to walk on. He could relax and think his ain thochts noo that he wasnae gart make polite conversation onie mair.

"Cheerio Jack, maybe see yis both later." Jack walked on doon the Blackfort Road on the same side as the buses were coming. Breaking into a trot past where Northdyke Street crossed the Blackfort, he soon reached the stop fornent Samoa Street, where the Gambles leeved.

Lily was waiting back frae the queue in a shop doorway. The arrangement suited Jack weel, for that was the "th'ee-dee" stage, in auld money and auld fares, and even if he got the bus to work every day, it would still only cost him 50p a week.

Lily gien Jack an exaggerated look o impatience.

"Ye'll be late for yer own funeral. I was near for goin' on maself." She was wearing a headscarf like all her friends did going to work. But in Lily's case it was to hide the fact that she, and she alone, hadnae her hair in curlers. They joined the queue thegither and watched the first few trolley-buses swish by athoot slowing doon ava. Whiles, scores o buses passed that were ower full for stopping, and as each bus passed, Jack looked alang the faces keeking out o the windows o the lower deck. He was looking oot for Walter. Despite the fact that Walter was a gye serious wee man, he aye made Lily giggle when he raised his hat and waved it til them as if he was in a State Procession. Mair often than no but, Walter had to wait just as lang for his bus as Jack and Lily.

As sometimes happened, on this particular morning they all ended up on the yin bus. Walter got up to gie his seat to Lily and they all kept silent company as the trolley bus glided and clicked its way doon the road. Jack gripped the cold steel seat back to keep his balance as the bus sunk like a lift. They had reached the steeper incline where the Blackfort and Cherryhill Roads intersect. His mind kept drifting back to his worry aboot losing his job. As they neared the city centre, Walter smiled his goodbyes and got off at his stop onto yin o the busy, wider footpaths that characterised downtown Bigganreek. Lily nudged Jack to watch for the antics o Walter and the wee pantomime he liked to do for them. As the bus took off, Walter would run alongside holding his hat off his heid in yin hand, and waving wae the other. When the bus got too fast for him to keep up, he pretended to trip up by deliberately catching his toe agin his heel, and flew forwards in a mock stumble wae arms flailing the air. Nae matter the many times Walter performed that routine, Lily hooched wae lauchter.

"Wud you luk at yer wee man theday agane – he'd affront ye."

Jack forgot his troubles for the moment and lauched too. "He's not wise, Walter. He's all right but. He used to conduct ye know. In fact he does yet."

"Conducts what? Buses, bands or lightnin'?" Lily asked wae a smile. Jack lauched again.

"Bands – he takes Cherryhill Silver."

"Themuns wi' the red jackets? I always take ma dead end

at them. The' luk like the fire brigade comin' down the road, so the' do. A must keep ma eye out for Walter the next time they're out."

"Ay but Walter doesn't go out wi' them when they're walkin' – he just takes them for contests an' the like."

"Just as well," Lily replied, "for if he seen somebody in the crowd he'd have the whole band tripped up in a heap."

Jack didnae say ocht for a bit, and Lily added, "A suppose Cherryhill'd be a high-class sort o' a ban' then?" She had a sparkle in her ee and Jack could see she was teasing him. Lily was easy to talk to, thocht Jack, even first thing in the morning. She sometimes just chatted on and, especially this morning, she was just the tonic Jack needed.

The last stretch o the walk through the Brickworks district, to the factory entrance, aye pit Jack in mind o ganging to watch a football match on the other side o the railway lines. Everybody was heading as fast as possible in the yin direction, wae a single destination in mind. As Jack and Lily turned doon Utopia Street, past the grand, but closed, director's entrance to the factory, the lang gangly figure of "Deke" Davison caught up wae them frae behind.

"How's the young lovers then, eh?" Deke said as he put his arms roon baith their shoulders and stuck his grinning grease-ball o a heid between them.

"Get aff, wud ye," Lily said with some annoyance, pulling herself away.

"Gie us a feg, Deke," Jack said. He quite liked the over-friendly way Deke always was wae him. It reminded him o a playful puppy, the sort you could neither ignore nor dislike. That didnae mean that Jack wanted his intrusive company just then but. A request for a cigarette would be certain to do the trick.

"A'm sorry, that's the last one A have," Deke said, stepping back to stub out his butt on the footpath. He had a justified reputation for aye being on the scrounge, and never offering any o his ain smokes. When the boys gathered in the toilets for a drag, Deke had this trick he liked to perform. It involved putting a cigarette in his mooth and, wae yin hand, he could strike a match in his pocket afore bringing it oot to licht up. It was generally believed that this was the first step towards, some day, producing a cigarette frae his pocket ready lit.

They reached the entrance gate at 7.53 am, or just before, for that was the time on Jack's clock card as he put baith his and Lily's back on the rack. Safe eneuch, as 8 was the dreaded digit. If the time was even 8.01, they would each lose half-an-hour's pay. Old Moiley Jackson, the stores foreman, came forrits frae his group of peers to check the names on the cards Jack had returned. He held onto Jack's shoulder and peered at the names on baith cards like a ticket inspector. Jack wasnae supposed to clock in mair than the yin card, but Moiley didnae mind as long as it was obvious he was on the look-out for anybody ava on the fiddle.

"See ye dinner time," Lily shouted abane the rattle o workers clocking in. The soond was like football turnstiles counting in the faithful. Jack took his ain road towards the stores. Halfway there he turned roon to wait for Lily's brother Billy. There was nae great friendship – or antagonism – between the twa o them, but they did maintain a sort o polite formality, the sort that was normal between a brother and his sister's boyfriend.

"Lily sez Mister Colin was lukin a word wi' me theday?" Jack said.

"A wud'n worry yer head about it, oul haun – more'n likely he's jist lukin' to check if ye've joined the Guild yet."

"A hope that's all it is," Jack said.

The Guild of Fleshers and Fowlers was the mutual benefit

society in question. It was the richt yin for Jack's job, and even if it was only a minor guild, it was one o a loose federation headed by the elite "Hammermen." The Hammermen were the all-powerful members o the Guild of Bricklayers, Carpenters, Masons and Plasterers, and so influential were they as a body that anybody o standing in the secondary Guilds was likely to be elevated to their ranks. So it was wae Mr Colin, and so it was that Mr Colin wouldnae hae kent that Jack had been initiated into the "F and Fs" in his first week at the factory.

Only a handfu o men wrocht in the loading bay alang wae Jack – there was Lily's brother Billy, Mr Jackson the stores foreman, Danny Burke the cleaner, twa mair youngish lads (Eric Mackey and Sidney M'Cann), and the somewhat sinister Joe Stitt.

"A hear oul Wetheral wants to see you theday," Joe Stitt said to Jack, turning on a cruel smile when he saw the discomfort on Jack's face. He rarely spoke to Jack, and never gien him a normal smile.

"Don't forget an' let us know if he asts ye about the Guild meetin'," he added.

"But A thought Mister Colin and the rest o' the Wetherals was all in the Guild?" Jack inquired innocently.

"Ay, maybe, if ye cud trust them. But I'll be the judge o' that."

Joe Stitt was the Warden of the factory's Chapter of the Guild, and as a sort of shop-steward he had a privileged position on the shop-floor. The most obvious privilege was, as far as Jack could see, that he didn't have to do any work unless he felt like it. Naebody, not Jackson nor Mr Colin, telt Joe Stitt what to do.

During the morning's wait, Mr Colin strode through the loading bay without stopping. He nodded a hello to Jack in a friendly way, which seemed like a good sign, but by dinnertime he still hadnae been sent for.

When Jack crossed the inner courtyard o the factory to the canteen, he didnae much feel like the sandwiches made frae Saturday's breid. The men had their ain eating area in a bare side room, wae forms roon the edge and a tennis table at yin end. Some went in for to buy a hot dinner at the food counter next door where the women sat at tables.

"A think A'll get masel a bite o' stew next door," Jack said to Danny.

"A wud'n bother, friend, she'll be just like water on a Monday," Danny advised. "Ye'd be better gettin it near the en' o' the week when she's thickened up."

Danny was something o an expert when it came to food. He never brocht a packed lunch – just twa flasks. By now Jack had got used to the spectacle o Danny going into the canteen to get himsel a dish, a cup and a knife and fork. When he apened the second flask, the yin without the tea, he shook the contents oot onto his plate. It was aye a bit reluctant to emerge – his carefully sliced and folded fry. Hardest to get oot was a rolled up potato farl, but once this had been winkled out wae a fork, a final shake would reveal a carefully rolled up fried egg. The egg always seemed alive as it unrolled itsel automatically on the plate and shimmered like a jellyfish.

"How cud ye ate that fry when it's not dead yet?" this voice asked frae behind a polite sandwich. "It wud make ye a vegetarian."

Jack left most o his piece untouched, and went to the canteen door to see if Lily was done yet. She was waiting for him with her coat on.

"Have ye seen Mister Colin yet?" she asked, as they started out to hae their usual wee dander along the shop-fronts. It was only about twenty yards frae the factory gate oot onto the Main Street o the Brickworks district.

"Na – well A seen him, so A did, but he hasn't sent for me yet."

By noo Jack was less concerned getting aboot the prospect. He was gye and sure that whatever it was, he wasnae for losing his job or ocht like that.

The afternoon was well on afore Jack M'Clean was cried into the office o the factory's Quality Manager. Six lang sennichts had passed frae Jack had started wae the Ulidican Food-Processing Company. It was a family run firm that had put generations o meat products into tin cans. The meats all looked the same as they sludged their way along the conveyor belts, but every sae often the Quality Manager would come oot o his glass-partitioned office to order a change o labels on the tins.

"Mister Colin" was the youngest of the Wetheral family involved in the business, so he felt it was important to prove hissel wae the workers in his new job. If the labels were getting switched to those o a well-known quality brand, Mr Colin would try to make a science oot o the job. A job everybody else knowed a well-trained monkey could do. He came oot wae his white coat and hat on like a cricket umpire. Under his oxter was the ever present clip-board, flapping wae blank sheets o scrap paper. At the food-line he picked up a random chunk o moving meat, smelt it, squeezed it, and then threw it back with a decisive signal to the foreman.

Once the necessary adjustments had been made, the canning-line foreman walked through a back door to the loading bay to get Jack.

"Mister Colin's lukin ye up in the office right away, M'Clean."

All the nerves that Jack thocht he had under control surged back the minute he was actually sent for. The thocht occurred to him that it micht all be another practical joke. He had already been caught with the old standards – like being sent to the packing room to ask the head girl for a lang weicht to hold doon the scrap paper frae the cardboard boxes.

"Jist ast her for a long weight," he had been told on his second day there. When he went into the packing room he discovered to his embarrassment that it was full o girls. He did his best to look casual as the young girls whistled and hooched at him. He singled oot the heid packer at her high desk and shouted above the din the girls were making by banging their scissors on empty cardboard boxes.

"A was toul' tae get a long weight in here."

"Certainly, son," Margaret said with a friendly smile, "jist houl' on there a wee minute an' A'll away an' get ye it now."

Margaret disappeared for what seemed like an eternity. As Jack stood wae the girls still in near riot, he decided to pick on a shy good-looker to stare oot. That only had the worsening effect of sending her giggling friends into near hysterics.

Like an electric shock, it dawned on Jack that his mission had already been accomplished – he had been given a long "wait." To further shrieks and lauchs he tried to walk oot as slowly and as casually as his red neck would allow.

"Oh good, come in Jack and sit down," Mr Colin said.

Jack was doubly relieved – he was expected, sae it wasnae a practical joke, and the tone o Mr Colin's voice didnae suggest that he was in any sort o trouble aboot his work.

Colin Wetheral liked to think that he was well thocht o by his staff. He knew that it would be years afore he could hac half the knowledge about the business that the workers theirsels had, but he liked to show that he cared aboot their welfare.

"Mr Jackson tells me that you're getting on very well in

the stores department," he said.

"Thanks, Mister Colin," Jack responded with growing anticipation.

"Well, it's early days yet, but you're the sort of man we want to keep here at Ulidican. Do you like it here?"

"Oh ay," Jack replied. "I like the work and the crack's good too."

"I hear you've started going out with one of the girls in the packing department – Lily Gamble?"

"Yes?" Jack said slowly, "is there something …"

"Oh no," Colin laughed, "no problem at all – in fact I'm very pleased. She's a lovely girl."

"Look," Mr Colin continued, getting to the point o his personal interview, "Lily is a good worker too. I know you haven't been seeing her all that long, but if you do get round to wanting to set up home, I might be able to help."

"What way?" Jack speired.

"Well you know we own two streets of houses here right beside the factory. You can have the pick of them when the time comes, and for half rent … No – I'll tell you what, if it's Lily or any of the Ulidican girls that you marry, you can have your choice, rent free."

"That's very good of ye, Mister Colin," Jack said, "I'll keep it in mind."

He was very pleased with the offer, no that he had any notion o getting married for years to come, but he was pleased that he had been singled oot.

The good feeling of self-satisfaction didnae last long however. As soon as Jack got back to his place, Joe Stitt spoke to him directly for the first time.

"Did Wetheral make ye an offer o' a house?" he said. Joe Stitt had worked in the "loadenin" bay for years athoot interference. He communicated wae few people, and naebody, no even the foreman, ever crossed him.

"Ay, he did," Jack answered, taking Joe Stitt's conversation as a further milestone in his mastery of the art o being a good worker.

"Well take my advice, boy, an' steer clear o' that."

"What d'ye mean?"

"Onest the' have ye in one o' them oul houses, the' have ye, body an' soul. Ye'll be trapped here." Joe's comments didnae need an answer, and everything he said was delivered as he was turning awa. When he had an after thocht, he had to return to say it.

"An' another thing – we wud'n want tae see Lily Gamble or any wee girl from the Claw havin' tae flit down here."

Jack wasnae sure whether Joe Stitt was warning him no to get Lily pregnant, or whether he was just agin anybody moving oot o the Claw.

Mr Colin thocht that Jack and Lily was a guid match. They baith came frae the Blackfort Road district. He didnae appreciate that there was different side street localities on the Blackfort Road. The higher up the road, oot o town, the mair respectable the area. Jack's parents didnae like the idea o Jack marrying beneath himsel to somebody frae Samoa Street.

Mr Colin hissel lived richt at the heid o the Cherryhill Road, as did maist o the other Wetherals. This was richt oot o toun, where some o the biggest hooses in the city had been bigged.

As he drove down the Cherryhill Road each day, across the city centre to where the factory was, he could see the terraced rows of houses running off behind the shop fronts. On the left the streets ran across to the Blackfort Road, and on the right across to the Mossvale Road. His knowledge of the world behind the shops and churches was limited to the fact that the Mossvale side of the Cherryhill Road was alien territory. Not that he gave either politics or religion a second thought. The Wetherals were above all that nowadays. But even to him the Mossvale people weren't just folk of a different religion. They were the scary "other" army that must be avoided rather than confronted. In a self-righteous sort of way he took pride in the fact that he felt none of the instinctive, violent hostility to the area that the folk from the Blackfort Road seemed to have in their veins. The Wetherals were above all that nowadays too. Nonetheless, he always felt negative vibes when he found himself on the Mossvale Road. Here he knew he was politically and socially unacceptable, while on the Blackfort Road he was only socially uncomfortable. The idea that Jack and Lily had any social gulf between them would never have occurred to him.

Jack had a lot to think on after his talk wae Mr Colin. He had the sort o imagination that could conjure up nightmare alternatives for himsel. Like being gien the choice between keeping his job, or keeping Lily as his girlfriend. The mair it had transpired that the opposite was the case, that didnae stop Jack thinking it through – without coming to any conclusion, bar confirming to himsel that he wouldnae like to lose either.

"My da wud kill you if he knew what we were doin'."

Jack remembered Lily's words after a steamy but furtively grasped love-making session. He couldnae imagine Lily's father even losing his temper. Her brothers were a different kettle o fish but, and as for Joe Stitt …

Jack shuddered, for in his mind's ee he could see the cruel smile on Joe Stitt's face as he imagined him drawing a six-inch blade frae his inside pocket. How much money would it take to persuade Joe to take oot a contract on somebody? Maybe he would just do it for the pleasure. Everybody had their price, abane which you would never hae ocht to worry aboot again. Jack imagined what he would do if he suddenly got hold o thoosands o pounds. He and Lily would be set up in a place o their ain and never hae to make love wae yin ear and yin ee apen again. He could even gie up work, although he knew he would miss the crack. Loads o money would free them baith frae the trap that was the Claw. Mr Colin had nae need to worry – his family were rich and the only thing they were tied to was the Ulidican factory. Jack's mind wandered in a childish way to the amount o money needed to buy that sort o freedom. Those large sums were meaningless anyway. Like the bets he used to make at school – trillions, quadrillions o pounds, upped to the "biggest number in the world squared," which Jack could aye better by betting "that number plus one," and so on. If his girl-friend's da had only known, Jack was getting near to understanding thon concept o infinity Ernie was aye explaining.

At five to four, Jack went doon early to meet Lily at the time-clocks. He saw her standing wae her coat on but un-buttoned. It hung loose and yin end o her unfastened belt hung lower than the tither. Jack smiled his hello and slipped his hands inside her coat, roon her waist. Lily didnae take her hands oot o her pockets, but lauched as she stepped back. Just then Joe Stitt was coming up behind Lily on his way oot. He grabbed her under the arms to stop her bumping into him, and gien her a start. Lily looked back in anger and said, "Get off you."

Joe Stitt snorted a laugh as he clocked oot. He didnae care that his card would show the few minutes short o 4 o'clock.

Lily glared at Jack. "He touched me there, you know?"

Jack took a moment for that to sink in. What was he supposed to do oniehoo? If it had been done on purpose, it was probably meant as much an insult to himsel as to Lily. In the stampede to leave once the hooter had gone, Jack was saved by the bell.

As they sat silently on the bus, Lily sullenly stared oot o the window. Jack looked at her face and realised how important she was to him. She looked spectacularly handsome when she was annoyed, and Jack felt it to the point o pain when he saw her creating a distance between the twa o them. He kent then that nothing meant mair to him nor keeping Lily, no even his job if that choice had been required. He even thocht briefly that he could kill for Lily, if the candidate was to be some waste o space like Joe Stitt.

"A went to see Mister Colin theday," Jack said. He knew the conversation needed a jump start if the twa o them wurnae for falling oot. The statement was dramatic eneuch to hae the desired effect.

"Oh ay? An' what was he lukin'?" Lily asked with sudden interest. Jack hadnae really intended to say ower much that soon, but the occasion seemed to demand it.

"He sez A can have one o' the Ulidican houses fornenst the factory when the time comes."

"Oh ay, an' what time wud that be then?" Lily asked with the first hint of a smile during the journey.

"Time enough," Jack replied wae an answer in his smile too. "But there wud be a catch to takin' him up."

"A suppose them wee houses wud'n be good enough for you then?" Lily asked with a sting.

Jack turned to her and whispered, "It wud be good tae have a wee place where we cud be all by ourselves, wudn't it?"

Jack took Lily's hand in his and put them inside her near coat pocket. He could feel the pocket lining agin her soft body wae the back o his hand. Their looks met and Lily's bottom jaw dropped slightly as their minds met on the same subject. She wriggled in embarrassment after a minute and got up a fraction before she needed to, as the bus neared her stop. "Are ye gettin' off here too theday?" she said in nervous anticipation.

"Ay," Jack said, "A'll walk ye down the street a bit."

As they walked doon the first stretch o Samoa Street, Jack wondered what it would be like to live richt doon in the deep o the Claw. If Lily would marry him, it wouldnae really matter where they set up hame. Joe Stitt had said he could get them a wee place – but he would be doing it for Lily and the Gambles, no for Jack. In a sense, that made Jack mair easy in his mind, for he didnae want to be beholden to Joe Stitt or to Colin Wetheral. Yet his mother wouldnae like him even getting married to such a through-and-through Claw girl. She would go ape if he went to live doon the lower end. Maybe he would never fit in properly.

"How come Joe Stitt can dish out houses roun' here?" Jack asked Lily. She just shrugged her shoodhers. "He says he's well in wi' the big noises in the Council," Jack added.

"Huh, some Council," Lily retorted. "More like he fancies himself well in wi' the flute band."

But that's as much as she would say on the subject.

Chapter 2

Ernie's Engine

"See us inventors," said Ernie Gamble, coming into the parlour frae the back yard. He had a poker in his hand that he used as an extra wagging finger for pointing at his twa sons, "we don't like gettin' called inventors. We'd far rather get called problem-solvers."

Kenny looked at his brother and apened the corner o his mooth in a sneer. Everything his father said annoyed him. His stupid ideas, his stupid jokes, his broad Bigganreek accent. He took a real scunner at the way his father had said "far-rarr" instead of "far rather."

"I'd far rather borrow my father's car," Kenny whispered loudly to his brother Billy wae the exaggerated pronunciation, "A'd far rarr barra ma farr's car."

Billy was embarrassed wae Kenny's rudeness, but Ernie shrugged it off.

"Ay, an' a fellafellaffalarry," Ernie retorted, wae another Bigganreek Ernieism for "a fellow fell off a lorry."

Kenny winced, mair irritated than afore. Billy smiled at his dad. If anybody took the hand oot o Ernie, his da just joined in and made fun o himsel too.

"Kenny, are ye readin' that paper yer sittin' on?" Billy had his ain way o sticking up for his da. "It sounds like it, for yer talkin' out o' yer backside."

Ernie pushed between his twa sons that were sitting huddled up to the coal fire. Wae yin hand on Billy's shoulder, he pushed the poker into the depths o the fire and left it there. It was a hame-made poker, a simple, roon length o iron bent into a wee circle at yin end for a handle, and gently tapering towards the point. The poker had monie uses, a fact betrayed by the kinks and bends alang its length. Ernie used it as a lever, a skewer and, on this occasion, as a soldering iron.

When the poker wasnae missing frae the hearth, Billy would put it in the hottest part of the coals tae the point was pink-hot, stick it through the bars o the grate, and bend it. Then it had to be heatit and straightened again – hence its misshapen length. Kenny's diversion was to drum it cold on the hearth tiles, and drill and poke wae it at the grouting between the tiles.

"Don't be playin' wi' that poker now," Ernie said to them baith. Ernie Gamble was a jokey-on-the-outside but serious-on-the-inside sort o a buddy. He wasnae ower sensitive aboot what people thocht o him, but he did like his technical skills to be taen serious. A "big wean" was how his wife described him to all and sundry, and naebody took his mechanical know-how less seriously than her. Iris, in a good mood, thocht her husband's activities in the back-yard shed were just "footerin' about," a harmless pottering that kept him oot o the pub.

Afore he had come back in the house wae the poker in his hand, Ernie had been in and oot the back door. His latest project was on his mind when Kenny had guldered at him, "Da, what invention are ye at now?"

To put a name on ocht that Ernie made was difficult. He didnae mind showing it off yinst it was working, but he hated haeing to explain what he was ettlin at afore he had the hale thing worked out in his heid.

The problem being solved that day was a guid case in point. A "Racing Pigeon's Homing Alarm Bell" micht hae been a fit name for it. But all he was doing was rigging up this bell in the kitchen to gie him warning when his racing-pigeons had landit, for Ernie's other passion was pigeon-fancying. Cantilevered oot ower the back half o the yard was a blue and white striped pigeon loft, like something oot o a carnival – and near as big as the hoose itsel. Under part o the floor o the pigeon shed was Ernie's workshop, and between this and the ootside toilet there was apen wooden steps up intae the loft. Nae doot the pigeons, homing in frae some place like Cork, could spot their hame frae miles off. However, frae the grun', amang the ticht streets of red-fronted brick houses and high yard walls in the Claw, it wasnae easy for an owner to watch oot for his returning birds.

Whiles, minutes could count. Yinst Ernie had gone in the shed to find his prize pigeon back already. Cursing himsel for no checking the shed earlier, he slipped the race-ring off and put it in the stop-clock. Syne he fun' oot he had been bate into second place by just 20 minutes. He couldnae be sure how lang his ain pigeon had been back.

The cure was easy eneuch. This new way, a bell would "ping" in the working kitchen if a bird landed on the ledge in front o the loft openings.

The device was only partly successful, but. In heavy rain the bell would ping away saftly. This riz a negative Pavlovian response frae Iris. The bell to her didnae mean pigeons but rain. Her washing had twice the normal hazards when drying in the yard, what wae baith the rain and the pigeons. When, on the other hand, the pigeon-bell pinged loudly as intended, Billy would shout, "Da! Shap!"

The pigeon loft, or at least the back yard, was a bit like a shop, richt eneuch. The yard door wae the back entry was under the steps into the loft. Just as the front door was never closed withoot the key sitting in the lock, sae the back yard door was never bolted. Iris's friends, and even neighbours that wasnae friends, just came in the front. Only men on business came to the front door and gien it a knock. Ernie's friends came round the back into the yard and sat, yarned and exchanged fags under the pigeons. Twathree o them, the regulars, knew aboot the pigeon alarm bell, and would trigger it with a stick if Ernie wasnae aboot. Then Billy's "Da! Shap!" meant what it said, and Ernie would grab his packet of cigarettes frae the mantelpiece and scuttle oot.

Ernie Gamble was retired twa year. He had a roon, shiny, jolly face wae gleaming white teeth when he smiled – which was brave and often. His baldie heid shone too, and was fringed by a horseshoe o wiry grey hair. Frae the back it made him look like a medieval monk. Monks didnae wear checked shirts but, and Ernie aye did.

The next-door neighbour, on the side on doon the street, was Miss Burke – an elderly and doting spinster known to all as "oul ma Burke". Ma Burke had a daft idea that Ernie was sure eneuch a monk, or at least a papish, for in her mind pigeons and monasteries were inextricably langled, and Ernie's pigeon loft maun be his private chapel.

But that was just the Ernie who inhabited the back yard, when Miss Burke saw him frae her bedroom window. The Ernie she met in the street, on the other hand, had a family and wasnae the same body. No that Ernie minded Miss Burke's disapproving stares frae her back bedroom window. She had daft ideas about nearly everybody and went up and doon the street wae an empty shopping bag, talking to hersel. If a stranger came into the street, she would catch them by the elbow, point to some door on the other side and say, "See him in there. He's a dirty baste, so he is."

Since Kenny had gone to College, a great separation had grown between himself and everything in the Claw. All Ernie's ingenuity and genuine thirst for understanding, to Ken, was just embarrassing small-mindedness. Burke was sure that Ken was being trained for a priest. As far as what Ken thought of Miss Burke was concerned, well she was typical of what the Claw could do to poison the minds of all those who hadnae experienced his ootside world o buiks and college scarfs.

"Why do ye not get oul ma Burke to tell ye when yer pigeons is back?" Ken said sarcastically to his father. "I'm sure she sees them before yer oul bell has a chance to ping."

Ernie, despite his hurt at the strange, cruel humour his auldest son had developed, was prood o having sired the only college boy in the street.

"There's worse than oul Burke roun' here," Ernie said, "an' anyhow she takes more notice of my friends than the pigeons."

After a pause, interrupted by the factory horn from Green's Spinning Mill, Ernie fell back on his stock of corny jokes. "Hoots mon, as the Scotchie says, late agane."

The reality o the Gamble household was mair mundane nor ma Burke thocht. Ernie headed a family o five: the wife and three growed-up childer. All three were still living at hame with nae mair intention o leaving than the pigeons. When Ernie said he had twa sons, he aye said "Oh ay, an' the wife has a daughter as well." There was some truth in that division of the house into men and women, for Billy and even Ken were – like it or not – cast frae the same mould as their father, while Lily seemed just to be there for helping her mother.

"You and oul Burke would make a right pair," Ken said, no joking, but serious-like.

"Ay," Ernie smiled. "Ken, lad, if ye could solve all her

problems ye'd be smarter than me an' my pigeons put thegither."

Ken had this college friend he brocht hame. He was a ginger-haired lad cried Rabbie, frae somewhere in the country. From they were wee fellas they baith supported the "City" football club, and met up on Saturday mornings, lang afore the match. Robert detested cricket and rugby – or rather the people he associated wae sic sports. For all his new college ideas, Ken felt mair comfortable wae Rabbie than onie others in his year. Ilka Saturday morning, Rabbie taen the bus across the city frae his digs to Samoa Street to meet up wae Ken and Billy. The three o them took a baa up to the park for a kick aboot afore getting ready to gang til the match in the afternoon. Rabbie liked going to the Gambles' hoose afore the match on Saturdays. He was daeing Chemistry or something, and Ernie imagined he was calling to see him too.

Robert hadnae a girlfriend, and liked to think that Ken's sister, Lily, had a bit o a notion o him. She aye seemed to be in the house when Rabbie was there, in and oot of the room wae her mother behind her or in front. Lily didnae look like a Bigganreek girl, never mind a Gamble, thocht Rabbie. He was fixatit wae her lips. They were fu, curvaceous, pouting and seemed only designed for kissing. Mair like Bridget Bardot's, than the thin, severe lips he was used tae. Would they still be like that when Lily was married, and middle-aged? When Ken noticed the vibes between Lily and Rabbie, he made sure he asked his sister aboot her boy. "Ye seein Jack thenight?"

"Ach him," Lily would say, and smile at her mother. Iris would then catch Rabbie's eyes moving from person to person, trying to read the situation.

No many friends o Billy's or Ken's would be gien their dinner at the Gambles, but Iris had the pan on in the working kitchen, making a fry for her sons and Rabbie afore they went to the match.

"What d'ye call thon wee lad – Rabble or Rebel?" Iris asked her son, pronouncing both words the same.

"It's Rabbie, ma, I toul ye before."

"Cud ye take ano'er egg, Rabble?" she asked from the parlour door wae the frying pan in her left hand and the pan flipper in her richt.

"Na thanks, Miss Gamble, wan's plenty enough," Rabbie replied.

Ken felt threatened wae Rabbie's gieing his sister a guid looking ower. No that he thocht he was jealous nor naethin. Sure the twa o them had got off wae a girl apiece at the college dance – and yin to spare, for there was three o them. Rabbie had clicked wae this college girl frae the kintra, but Ken's was real high-class. Yvonne, they called her. Never lastit lang but. They didnae want to gang oot unless it was a foursome, an then they were aye looking for another fella for their friend.

Billy came oot o the working kitchen into the front kitchen parlour wae his plate piled high wae fried soda and pritta breid. Ken followed wae twa similar plates and handit the richt-hand yin tae his friend. Lily fistled in behind with an apron-fu of knifes and forks, and put a set on the table at the window for Rabbie.

"C'mon up to the table, and sit down," she invited. Rabbie obeyed as the others sut roon the fire. Ernie brocht his mug o tea frae his ain seat and sat down opposite Rabbie at the table.

"Who's playin' theday, then?" Ernie said, and without waiting for an answer said, "Ye can always rely on City, that's one thing for sure, for the'll always let ye down!"

Rabbie liked Ernie. He was always disappearing into the back yard and coming back smelling of oil and iron filings. In the same way that Ken resented his friend taking an interest in his sister, he also resented Rabbie's obvious interest in his father's mysterious, mechanical adventures.

"What's yer da makin' out the back?" Rabbie speired after another o Ernie's disappearances.

Ken smiled, despite himsel, at Billy's non-committal repone. "He's forgin' 10p coins for slot machines. He just files the corners aff 50p bits."

Ernie, in fact, was starting into a machine that could detect underground running water – in leaks or in pipes. He would hae loved to hae shown it to somebody wae a college education like Rabbie, but now wasnae the time. Oniehoo, everything else he had made had worked, after a fashion, withoot any such help.

"It'll never float," Rabbie joked to Ernie when he appeared again.

"What's that son?"

"Thon oul contraption ye're makin' out the back."

"Ach ay," Ernie lauched heartily, "that's what the' said about the Titanic."

"Na," Billy said, "they said she was unsinkable."

"Ay, right enough," Ernie lauched again. "A better do better than that, then."

City Fitbaa and Athletic Club was bidding for the league and cup double again. Their hame grun' wasnae all that far frae where Rabbie was living, but he preferred plundering through the city centre to and frae the match wae the rest o the herd.

Rabbie and Billy, like the rest o them, wore supporters' scarves, the standard blue yins wae black and red stripes running straucht or diagonally across. Ken, aye the odd yin oot, had a serge college-type scarf wae the black and red stripes running the length o it, which he kept folded up in a drawer in his bedroom. Whiles, Ken didnae even wear his scarf to the matches, but he put it on theday, for he was impatient to get oot o the hoose.

"What's the time now?" Iris asked when she seen the boys getting ready to go. "Sure yis're far too early."

Rabbie sat doon again on the sofa alangside Billy. While they sat quiet, wae naebody talking, the clock on the mantelpiece seemed to tick louder and louder.

The silence was noticeable all the mair for the stranger in the hoose. If he had been yin o the family he could hae just sat there reading, or staring intae the fire, lost in his thochts. He didnae try to make conversation, but run his eyes roon the room frae object to object. Iris was uncomfortable wae the silence and went oot to the kitchen, wae Lily following her. Nae matter the much Rabbie's presence in the hoose was welcome, he was still a guest rather than a friend. He had the benefit o a college education, like Ken, and that was something special to Ernie at least. Ken, however, was Ken, despite his education. Buik-learning didnae wipe oot his past. He was, and would aye be, Ernie Gamble's lad frae Samoa Street. "Ye ken oor Ken, as the Scotchies say," Ernie would answer a neighbour's speirin aboot his studies, "the only book that's right is the one he's readin'."

Ernie saw Rabbie was studying him, or rather his bricht yellow checked shirt wae rolled-up sleeves. The sleeve rolls showed a reverse pattern of red and black cross stripes on an off-white backing that clashed with the front.

"Now, I'm not one of yer ignorant masses, Robert," he said suddenly. "You would know all about evolution an' all? We're all relatit til monkeys, ye know. Wait till I tell ye – A seen this dead dog wi' its guts hangin' out. It had a wee liver an' all the same workin' parts that we have. A seen it wi' my own eyes, an' I think all them animals just works the same way we do."

"Oh ay, Mr Gamble," Rabbie started to reply, "ye wouldn't have to tell somebody from the country that."

Ken stood up again, putting his scarf back around his neck for the second time.

"C'mon Rabbie. We better get on."

Ernie stood up, raised his empty tea mug again to his mouth, threw his heid back to drain the last drop, and banged it down as he let out his breath loudly. "Better get on maself," he said as he checked his side wisps of hair in the looking-glass ower the fire. As the lads trooped out the front door, Ernie came back to the mirror to check his shirt. Iris had seen Rabbie looking at it too. "Thon oul shirt o' yours is boggin'," she said. "Away an' get it changed."

"A'm workin' am't A?" Ernie answered, still checking the buttons in the mirror. "A'll change whenever A'm done."

The yellow checked shirt was Ernie's favourite. When he was young he told his friends he could work out the colours of the checked shirts cowboys wore in the pictures. In those days the cowboys did wear checked shirts, but the pictures were in black and white. All you needed, Ernie said, was to know what the real colours were like in a photo. Every shade o grey stood for a particular colour. "Thon one's blue, an' yer mon at the back has a yella one on," Ernie would tell his mates at the matinee. Naebody doubted him, but just in case, he would add, " – an' A've niver been proved wrong yet." So colour movies held nae charm for Ernie. Likewise, he had nae interest ava in modern, purpose-made gadgets bocht in a department store.

Oot in the shed, Len Bones was sat waiting. When Ernie came oot and apened the door, the cigarette smoke hung in layers.

"Ach, billie Len," Ernie said, surprised to see him sitting there. He only called when he was looking something, and Iris didnae like him about the place ava.

Len nipped his cigarette oot between his thumb and first

finger and blew the black end oot. Then he tapped it firm and put the three-quarter butt into his breist pocket.

"Ye in themorra?" he asked, standing up.

"Ay, we're niver out on Sundays."

"See ye then," Len said and went back oot into the entry leaving shed and yard doors apen.

Len Bones had got a start in the shipyard the same week as Ernie, over 40 years ago, but it didnae last a month. Frae then he was the local coalman, dealer and hood – sometimes separately, whiles all three at once. The minute he was startit in the Yard he was thieving, or sae it was believed. You could aye tell what colours the latest ship was to be done oot in – just by walking up Brackenridge Street where the Bones's leeved. At quitting time, the gate security kept a watch out for Len as he came through with a barrow-load of assorted rubbish – empty paint tins, wooden scraps, shapes frae the pattern shop, and broke electric fittings. Security checked each piece agin permission dockets frae the foremen. They were sure he was up to something. It was three weeks later – and fifteen new wheelbarrows – afore they finally cottoned on.

When Ernie and Iris was first married, afore Ken was born, Len was then their coalman. It was Len that put Ernie up to his first production as the street's unofficial scientist. The city was in a high state of tension, and real danger beset the Claw. Whenever the later troubles got discussed in the Gamble hoose, Iris would say to Billy and Ken, "See the fightin' now, that's nathin'. When we were first married, yer da an me, there was real troubles then." Ernie smirked, and the boys seen it coming.

"Ay," Ernie agreed, "an' it was even worse out in the street."

Ernie's first piece of technical ingenuity was a street siren. It was a sort o community burglar alarm that he mounted on the top gavel o the terrace when the stanes and bare-knuckle rioting of those days came too close for comfort. Len Bones had the idea, and then Ernie produced it. Ernie near got a bad reputation when Len let the siren off regularly on false alarms, so he disowned it when the neighbours complained.

"Don't you have no more dealin's wi' thon bad oul skitter," Iris had said. "His heart's as black as his face." Mobility drills, Len called them.

"Ach, Len's not that bad now."

"Luk, Ernie Gamble, the polis'll niver be out o' our house, if ye keep his company." When Iris used Ernie's full name, even in those early days, that was the last word. But Len was back, much to young Iris's annoyance. He offered the Gambles free coal for as long as they needed if Ernie would work on a specialist job for him. He wouldnae hae to dae it in his ain back shed. Everything he would need was already up in the coal-yard. Ernie wisely took naethin to do wae it. But Len had smiled when Ernie said no. That was aye a bad sign.

"The price o' coal's goin' up steep themorra – for you anyhow Ernie."

Len Bones's fixed smile signalled the end of coal deliveries for the Gambles, for he had bullied himself a monopoly in that part o the Claw. Even back in those days, Len Bones was the only acquaintance Ernie didnae crack his wee jokes to.

Necessity was aye the mother o invention, so Ernie had started his second engine in the back yard. Basically, it was a glorified waste-paper shredder, mulcher and press. He experimented by mixing pigeon dung, waste oil and other things wae the paper mash tae he got the richt mix to mould, press and dry into burnable "fire breeks." Apart frae the mildly nauseous smell frae the hearth when the fire was in full blaze, Ernie's machine was regarded as a local marvel. "Particularly suitable for ranges." Ernie had his slogan ready, but naebody would buy ocht but Len Bones's coal.

O coorse there was other inventions doon through the years – but it was thocht by the hale street that it was the same machine every time, wae a few minor adjustments and extra parts. Iris had jist yin concern each time a new project was under way. Had Len Bones ocht to dae wae it? In his mair mature years Len was still a furtive, sleekit sort o a body. But he had never really been catched oot at ocht serious enough to land him in jail. If it was true that he was "involved," you could be sure it was naethin to dae wae religion or politics on Len's part. A raw tribalism maybe, but if badness was aboot, Len Bones was bound to be mixed up yin way or another.

You would never hae taen Mal Bones to be Len's brother. They looked a bit alike – thin and dark haired – but there the similarity endit. Mal was married, hard-working and honest, and Len was nane o these. Frae he had been married, Mal had leeved at the laich end of Samoa Street, near the junction wae Captain Street. His house was the local barber's shop, but had neither striped pole nor name boord to mark it oot. For years he had cut hair in his front parlour. In them days, the way you knew his house was to find the pair o buffalo horns that looked oot frae the back of the porch, through the apen front door. When Mal took ower the hoose next door, he convertit it into a proper barber's shop wae big mirrors, and twa second-hand barber's chairs. On Saturdays, when it was extra busy, Mal had another barber help him out. This was George, a big stout redfaced man that took twice as lang ower a haircut as Mal did. Boys and men mixed on the forms roon the wall as they waited their turn. Mal kept the conversation going – no tae the person he was working on – but tae all the waiting customers. George didnae say much, but lauched and nodded in enthusiastic agreement with everything Mal said.

"Go on, Mal, give them a magic trick," George would ask Mal with his eyebrows up and nodding a "yes, go on" tae his ain suggestion. Maist o Mal's tricks were short, sharp disappearing tricks with matches or coins. They were over in a flash and he returned to his clip-clip-clipping scissors, ignoring all appeals of "Go on, Mister Bones, give us another," or "Go on, Mister, how did ye do it?"

Whiles other customers would join in with a few tricks o' their ain, and George would gie a lauch. "Did ye see that one, Mal? He'll be cutting the hair next."

George was frae Primrose Street richt at the end o the Claw, and a top man in the Kindly Order o Guild Provincials. It seemed he knew everybody, and the roaring trade done on a Saturday at Mal's Barber's shop had something to do wae George's presence.

Ernie came every fortnicht for a special wet shave and a short-back-and-sides, as regular as clockwork.

"They'll have more to brush up after yer shave than yer haircut," Iris told him.

"Ay," said Ernie; "they're gonna start up a baldies' discount club."

A debate started up in Mal's anent water divining, and whether or no there was ocht in it. Ernie took the view that there was, and that there had to be some scientific principle behind it. O coorse he could prove it.

There wasnae muckle scope for water-divining in Bigganreek, sae George said he kent this man in the country that could sink wells and divine water with a wee bit o stick. Wae his heid still reeking o bay rum, Ernie got stuck in straucht off to his latest engine. It was, at heart, a simple electric conductivity meter – on the notion that underground water conducted electric – but his test runs in Samoa Street threw up twa problems. Yin was that underground pipes produced the same readings whether they carried water or no. The simple remedy for this would be to add a metal detector.

The other problem was that his tests had attractit the interest o Len Bones. Whether innocent or no, Len's interest aroused, in turn, the suspicions o Ernie's wife and family. To try and stop Ernie in fu flight, however, was as futile as trying to make the Blackstaff Water flow back up the mountain.

"Bout ye, Digger."

"Ach, billie Ken."

Digger spun round from his position at the front o the bus queue on the Blackfort Road.

"Yis aa for the match?" His question didnae need an answer, for Ken, Billy and Rabbie were all sporting red, black and blue City colours – alang wae a thrang o others standing at the "fitbaa special" bus stop.

Digger stayed in his place until the double-decker trolley bus came. There was standing room only and he hung on the upright chrome bar at the back platform tae the others had squeezed on board. The trolley bus was excitedly quiet as the men watched oot the window. Apart frae the soond o the tyres treading doon the Road, there was just the soft whine o the electric motor. Everywhere was shoppers wae clumps o City supporters bashing their way through them on the fitpads. A pint-sized man standing towards the front o the bus broke the silence as he opened up a general conversation in a whiney, fruity voice. He was ower-decoratit in City's colours, including a striped duncher. And he pronounced all his s's as "sh."

"Shee theesh oul tralley-bushes, niver enough room, sho there'sh nat," he nyerped. Everybody looked oot the windows, in case he was talking to them, and the silence grew deeper as the bus sped by each stop.

"Stupid, puttin sheats in a futba speshil – eh?" the wee man asked the backs o an array of heids. Billy and Rabbie catched each other's een and tried no tae lauch. They looked awa quick.

"What did ye get for yer dinner theday Rabbie," Digger asked, "shaushages?"

"Shut up you," Ken growled, under his breath.

"Don't mention the match," Billy said smirking. "I don't want to know what team he shupportsh."

"There'sh just one team can win the double now, sho there ish," the wee man announced, looking roon him for an acknowledgement that somebody was listening.

Digger nudged Ken wae his elbow. "Messerschmitts at two o'clock," he said.

Ken answered. "Yes – City!" he said to the wee man, who looked at him intendy as if he never expected to get an answer.

"CI-TY! – thump, thump, thump, CI-TY! – thump, thump, thump."

Rabbie started up a chant on the bus. All the under 30s joined in. So did Digger imitating the wee man, and lauched.

"Ye shweatin' Ken?" Rabbie said. Ken didnae smile but looked oot the window.

The bus journey took 20 minutes frae Blackfort Road, across the city centre, to Biggan Park where the match was being held. Yinst fu, it didnae stop until it reached the corner o the Bigganreek Road where the railway brig came close to the gates.

Bottlenecked roon the turnstiles was a mass o grey figures, the hale tinged wae a purple hue – as it seemed. The red, blue and black colours o City merged frae a distance to gie this purple tinge. Some wore different combinations, maybe only twa o the three alang wae thin stripes o white. To maist, attending a match at "Jerusalem" or the "Holy City," as Biggan Park was known, was the nearest thing to a religious pilgrimage they would be likely to experience. A religious experience it was too. The club colours had deep, deep tribal meanings and a brave number o the supporters' sangs was sung to hymn tunes. Billy didnae know that, leastways no tae ma Burke had accosted him yin Saturday returning frae the match wae the rump o a singing, victorious rabble. "Ye'll burn in hell for changin' them words," she said.

Ernie and Iris, like near all the Prods in the Claw, never went near a church on a Sunday. Ernie wasnae in a band, and hadnae been near his Guild in years – so he was never even at a church parade or anything. But he knew the tunes that ma Burke had scolded Billy for using were originally hymn tunes – and still were, tae the gospel-greedy. And Iris had once grabbed playing cards off the table frae Billy and Ken, and bucked them in the fire, saying "Don't let me ever catch youse playin' wi' the divil's cards on a Sunday again." So they were Godly eneuch.

Yinst Billy had been wae the band at a Guild church parade, and joked after aboot "prayin' an' all" to Mal in his barber's shop.

"Don't ye believe in God, then?" was George's surprising question.

"Not at all, that's just for oul weemin."

"A thought ye said ye were a Protestant, but?"

"Bloody apt an' I am, like," Billy answered aggressively. It seemed to satisfy everybody but George.

Back at the match, Billy kent this was his religion. Like guid church-goers that had their ain pews, Billy and the gang aye stood at the same spot. It was about three-quarters up the terraces, at the goal end. Only a very ticht band o real roughs gathered richt ahint the goal. If you joined that crowd you micht weel end up in trouble. The lads' position was such that they looked doon frae abane the back left-hand-side o the other team's goal. It was their territory, where they would meet up wae other billies in a group o a dozen or so, maybe more, depending on how big the match was. This position was aye their ain – at either end, and at onie other ground.

In those days the hard core supporters changed ends at halftime, sae as they were aye encouraging their ain team as the wingers brocht the baa towards them. The fitbaa itself was different then too – naebody had heard of 4-3-3 formations or the like. The names o the positions were as fixed as the rules. Wae outside left, inside left, centre forward, inside right and outside right in the front row, and left back and right back in the back row, what way could you have ocht but a 5-3-2 line up? A forward wae a powerfu left foot made a good outside left as long as he could dribble as well. And vice versa on the richt wing. Ernie said if you couldnae kick with either foot, City would make you centre forward.

When Billy, Ken, Rabbie and Digger arrived at their ain iron stanshion in the terrace, it was still early. Jim Reid and Billy 'Skipper' M'Carroll were already there. The crush barriers were an awkward height for leaning on – higher than a shop counter, about chest-high. They were made o U-section steel, wae the flat edges painted wae bricht blue gloss paint. Ken took a pair of leather driving gloves out o his coat pocket, put them on, and proceeded to scoot some droplets of water off the top o the iron barrier.

"Nice gloves, Ken," Skipper said. "All ye need now's a car."

Ken's leather gloves and college-type City scarf annoyed Skipper. He thocht he looked dressed for the stand, no the terraces. Even mair annoying was the way Ken, and Ken alone, would clap when the opposition scored a goal at the other end. Amid the sickened silence at the City end could be heard the sound of Ken's leather gloves, whoomph – whoomph – whoomph, slowly signalling that he was a sport and was here to appreciate guid fitbaa. Nae real conviction there, they all thocht.

With ten minutes to go afore kick-off, the terraces were filling up all aroon. The lads' ain crush barrier could only take aboot five along it with everybody's arms spread out wing-like, elbow to elbow. The rest stood in a semi-circle behind. The sun suddenly came out and gave a new brichtness, catching the dapples o City colours sloping doon the terraces below.

Excitement was mounting and the buzz o the crowd meant that listening became part of the experience. Tommy M'Cune and a nameless billie arrived. Tommy had gone to Primary School with Billy and Ken in the Claw, before his family moved out to a new housing estate outside the city boundary. Close behind them, pushing down from the top of the terraces, came Billy 'Herbie' Herbison wae an auld man, noticeably no wearing a City scarf. He turned out to be Herbie's uncle, over frae the north o England somewhere. Herbie's uncle stood at the back o the bunch, slightly nervous o the strange surroundings.

"About the size of one of our 3rd Division crowds, this," he said. It turned out that was how he rated the standard of football too. Later he revealed that his hame team in Lancashire was in the 4th Division, sae his comparison didnae seem that bad.

Ken was chatting politely to Herbie's uncle when a thunderous roar shook their rib-cages. The teams, City and Ballypeden United, had taen the field. It was like the first exciting plunge on a roller-coaster.

City scored three goals that match, and Ballypeden didnae get a look at the baa. The excitement was mair on the terraces than on the pitch. Nae need to watch the match closely, but singing, chanting and scarf waving took over. "Ais–ey! Ais–ey!" Hymn tunes with tribal, triumphant words. More like real religion. It moved souls. Billy, Digger and the rest of their billies were carried away on a blood-thumping high that was worth fechting for. And wha wouldnae? Billy thocht on the hymn tunes and church-going for a minute – the tunes micht be the same notes, but you had to be here to be stirred by them. How could you fecht and die for something that couldnae keep you awake on a Sunday morning? He smiled as he thocht o George in the Barber's shop – being teased that the Guilds should be banned from parading to church.

"I didn't fight and die in two World Wars to let that happen," he snapped.

"Hula!" – "Hula!" – "Hula!" The crowd roared as they revelled in the savage reputation they had. Journalists thocht that this chant was a cocky assertion of hooligans, glorying in their bad reputation. It was a wee bit like that, but it had been started by supporters from Samoa Street, Lagos Street, Fiji Street and the other Jungle-Jim streets in that quarter of the Claw. It was just a bit o a joke, inverted pride in their low-status origins. Billy and Digger were as proud o haeing invented it as onie other achievement in their lives to date.

A final flurry o scarves and arms swept abane the crowd like a jig, as the dancing colours of the City supporters greeted the final whistle. They bubbled like the water at the fit o a waterfall, afore turning all as a mass and pouring oot the apen gates on to the feeder streets across the Bigganreek Road. Nae point in trying to get a bus back. Oniehoo the walk back across the city centre wae a chanting, yahooing mob was one of the best parts o the day.

"We are, we are, we are the billie-boys …" made a brave echo in the tall biggins o the city centre. "Billy-boys," or "billie-boys?" They all used to take it for "comrade billies," tae the media gien it the other, sectarian meaning. Well, better still if it made ye even mair macho.

"In for a bottle?" Digger turned to ask the rest as the

dwindling pack reached the Blackfort Road at last.

"Ay, try the Friesian Bull," Rabbie replied.

He had nae need o coming back that far but he enjoyed the inquest in the bar as much as the actual fitbaa. Tommy and the rest agreed.

"Ken. C'mon now," Rabbie encouraged Ken, wha looked unsure.

"Not the Bull, that's the bar m'da an his cronies drinks in."

"Sure he'll not be there at tea-time on a Saturday," Billy said, walking off in the direction of the Bull. Digger, Rabbie, Ken, Skipper and Jim Reid followed.

Compared to the fresh, sunny ootside, the inside o the Friesian Bull was dark and smelt of stale, spilt beer. There were only a few men drinking separately at the bar. Apart, that was, frae Len Bones sitting in a dark corner, by himsel, wae a wee roon table in front o him barely big enough for his ash tray, bottle and glass.

When the City billie-boys had gone through five or six rounds, the broon beer bottles filled the maist o the three small tables they were at.

Eventually Len Bones appeared at Billy's shoodher.

"Well lads, another big victory for the cause theday?"

"Ay, Len, did ye hear the score?"

Len didnae repone straucht away.

"Ye missed the trouble roun' the Pound then?"

"What was that?" Rabbie asked.

Again Len didnae gie an answer. He went back to his table, lifted his almost empty glass, and brocht it over to sit down beside Rabbie. Ken was uneasy, and sae was Billy.

"It's the herd instinct, ye see," Len mused. "Prods are supposed to be free-thinkers, but when they get in a herd, the herd instincts takes over."

Ken took the bait. "It's more like birds wi' their territory than animals in herds," he said.

Len took a drink from his glass, watching Ken as he did so.

"Yer da has more sense. Ye wud'n catch him stampedin' about wi' the herd."

"Wud ye like another bottle?" Rabbie asked Len.

He drained his glass without looking back and said, "Ay, on ye go son."

Ken looked at his watch. "I'll maybe get on home now for my tea."

"Tell yer da A'll see him themorra," Len said, making himself comfortable.

"He's got more brains than thon anyhow," he continued to Rabbie and Billy, nodding towards Ken as he went out the door, gloves first.

"Ach Ken's clever too," Rabbie said.

Len ignored him. "How's yer da's engine comin on?" he asked Billy.

"I don't know, sure A'm never in his shed."

"Well, tell him A'll see him themorra, then," Len said as he got up and took his glass and new bottle back to his ain corner.

Chapter 3

"Hambo" Jack

Hambo Jack was a scary, bull-neck o a man, wha aye looked like he was freeze-framed. Even in the street ootside his end hoose at the corner o Daisy Street and Gilbert Street he was rarely seen on the move – just standing, making his presence felt. He was in his late fifties wae close-cropped grey hair and folk said he had never been the far o the city centre for ower twenty year. When he was deid and gone, people micht call him a character. But noo he amused naebody. The only folk that talked to him were those, like Len Bones, that wanted to be seen as yin o his billies.

Mrs Jack had died from her injuries after a series of falls doon her ain stairs. That again was ower twenty years ago. "Accidental Death" was the Coroner's verdict, and the police said there was nae evidence o foul play. Whiles, Hambo would be seen at the Blackfort Road end o Gilbert Street, chatting and joking wae the polis when there was onie trouble on the Road. Folk wondered what for, as the polis were aye rude and short wae everybody else. But then sae was Hambo.

His dog used to like him. Yin day poor Jip was dug up by police on the waste grun' beside the band hall. He had been buried alive. Folk said that a gun had been buried there after a killing. Jip had gone and dug it up, sae it maun hae been Hambo Jack's. Anyhow, what else would the poor dog hae been deliberately buried alive for? That was all the polis ever fun', and that looked suspicious in itsel. But others said Hambo did dirty work for the polis in the first place.

Carla was Hamilton Jack's only dauchter. She was in her thirties and as ruch-looking as her father. Big too. Short, stocky legs and arms like bolsters. And this enormous bosom. "Used to play the cymbals in the band when she was wee," the boys joked, "but she had to give them up for technical reasons." Not that they would joke aboot her - or call her "Car Jack" – to her face.

Naebody had seen the inside o her hame. The front door was aye closed, and the front doorstep was yin o only twa or three in the street that was never scrubbed into a semi-circle oot into the fitpad. The windows were unmodernised 'wundaes' wae dirty, holey lace curtains across the inside o the bottom sash and dark green roller blinds abane. Baith could barely be seen through the dirt on the glass. Carla never had callers, or freens. Her trips to do the messages were aggressive guerrilla raids on the corner shop, and usually ended in an argy-bargy about something or other. Her other trips were to tell some poor body, "M'da's sent for you, so he has." These invited callers at Hambo Jack's didnae land at the front door, but roon and in the back yard. That door was never closed, no that there was muckle worth a-seeing for nebby neighbours. Wee lads, exploring the district, were far too afeard o Hambo Jack to even pass by the yard door. The other end of the back entry was for the public to use.

"Len, you're wantin' wi' m'da," Carla said to Len Bones at his front door in Brackenridge Street.

"Where, down at the house?"

"No, he's waitin' on ye in the pub."

The Friesian Bull was on the corner o the Blackfort Road and Antwerp Street – on the opposite side of the Blackfort Road to the Claw. It was a small corner building with everything roonded abane the door, including name boord, brick work and slated roof. It looked like a dinky wee roon gatepost, or a corner turret, for it was much wee'r nor the 3-storey shops fronting the Blackfort Road. The shape and age o it looked as if a quaint part o the back streets had escaped on to the main road. Another thing that made it seem old was the floor inside. It was way below the level o the fitpad ootside. There was twa steps doon into its dark, low gut.

Len Bones came doon the twa steps, his lungs peching like bellows at a kindling fire. His throat was burning too, but no wae thirst.

"Hambo Jack about?" he asked the barman.

The only response was a shrug o the shoodhers. The barman was a mean git – a tall thin vulture wae roonded shoodhers and a craning neck. He never said much or appeared to take notice o ocht. His face was thin and sharp. His furtive, aye-looking-the-other-direction een couldnae baith be seen at the yin time. This was acause o a beak-like neb to match his vulture-like shape.

"Fix Len a bottle o' plonk there, Deke," said Andy Dougan. "I'm waitin on Hambone masel," he explained to Len. The mair Andy was sitting at the bar, whilk ran doon the length o the lang narrow room, Len taen his empty glass and bottle o export to his corner seat. Andy, a lanky affable chap whase reputation as a hard man came frae the bad company he kept, brocht his ain drink ower and sat doon wae Len.

"What d'ye think Hambone wants us for?" Andy said, studying Len's poker face carefully.

"Wouldn't you just like to know?" Andy's anticipation increased.

"So you know, do ye?"

"I've a good idea," Len lied.

Andy wasnae a bad sort at hairt. He had been in trouble but. No that he would start a fecht, but he was aye the next to join in. And he'd been in jail. A short, daft episode when his mother even got a minister to speak for him in coort. He said he was easy led, for there had been three o them at the robbery at the corner shop doon Solomon Street. Andy had an imitation gun. Actually it was a black replica Luger water-pistol. When the hoose door o the shop was answered, the other twa ran away and left Andy there by himsel.

"Yer money or yer life," he demanded.

"Well, ye better take ma life, for A'm not givin ye no money."

So Andy let him have it, right between the eyes. His cronies still sniggered at Andy filling the pistol up wae water afore the job. He appeared in court wae his arm in a sling, for the shopkeeper had broke his arm in return. But that was naethin to what he would hae got if he had said ocht aboot others being involved.

In through the low double-doors, and doon the twa steps, came Hambo Jack. He stood there checking wha was in the bar. Andy went to stand up, either to greet him or to buy him a drink, but Len tugged him back doon by the tail o his coat.

The barman gien yin o his rare, sneering smiles, but didnae meet Hambo's een. He reached up for a glass and started fixing him a pint o porter. Hambo Jack didnae acknowledge Len or Andy but walked doon to the end o the bar where a panelled door led oot o the back. Late drinkers were let oot this way into Antwerp Street, oot o the obvious eyes o the polis on the Blackfort Road. The barman left down the pint o porter to settle, and scuttled sideways, like a crab, doon ahint the bar in front o Hambo. He reached doon a rim lock key frae a high shelf corner, and apened the back door, nodding Hambo through, yet no looking near him. Behind the door was a set o stairs, leading to rooms abane the bar, and at their foot, the door leading oot into the street. The inner door was closed behind Hambo, and the barman finished pulling the pint. After a minute, he took it over and set it on the small table in front o Len and Andy.

"Can I pay for Hambone's pint?" Andy asked. The barman shut his een and shook his head slowly.

"C'mon you," Len said, lifting his own and Hambo's drink. "Up the back. An' A toul ye, quit callin' him Hambone."

Hambo Jack's reputation as a vicious street fighter was past history. No for years had he ever been involved in yin himsel. They said he was like a volcano, and you never kent when he would erupt. Nae warnings. If he was annoyed in the old days, he would wait for weeks, and then spring at his victim, completely without warning. Whiles he selected his victim athoot guid cause. The suddenness was just the same. It was this unpredictable violence that gien him the reputation as the hardest man in the Claw. Naebody ever crossed Hambo Jack and survived. And he owed favours to naebody.

Twenty minutes after the rendezvous in the Bull had started, it was over. Len had taen Andy straucht oot the side door into Antwerp Street and away. Hambo Jack came back into the bar and sat doon in Len's corner seat lang eneuch for Deke the barman to bring him another pint.

"How's yer ma this weather?" he asked Deke, almost warmly. Deke's mother, a short stoot woman in her seventies, was the real owner o the bar, but only turned oot to help her son on rare occasions.

"Nat too bad, Mr Jack," Deke replied. As polite conversations went, this was a lang yin for baith men. Neither looked at the other. Deke's een were aye on his work, no on the customers – or sae it seemed. Hambo constantly watched others ower the shoodher o whaever he was speaking to. His een glared a silent "What do you think you're lookin' at?" to all. Other times and he would seem in a guid mood, even haeing a bit o crack with some of the regulars. But in the middle o a joke, when all were belly-laughing including himself, he would instantly turn, banging his nieve on the table and pointing a finger at an unsuspecting member o the company. It kept them all on edge. And, if there was any trouble anywhere, scores o men would say that Hambo Jack was definitely in the Friesian Bull at the time o the 'incident'.

He wasnae a cruel man, Hambo Jack. So said ma Burke. She thocht if he was half the villain he was made oot to be, he would be living in a big hoose in Southcity, alang wae the rest o the crooks and bigwigs. The fact that he leeved in yin o the dirtiest hooses in the street was evidence enough for her that he was a man o principles. That was, the dirtiest hoose as far as Gilbert Street was concerned.

The maist mingin hoose in Samoa Street was where the poor Bates brothers had leeved. Their hoose was like a fossil, unchanged frae their father died in 1916 at the Somme. Like a scene frae Great Expectations, the mother had gone clean oot o her heid, no letting ocht be touched. Eventually she was taen awa after trying to torch the hoose with the twa boys sleeping upstairs, and hersel holding a photograph o her deid Stanley. He was in uniform – no o the 36th Division that he died in, but an earlier yin o him in the Fire Brigade ambulance team.

The boys were a bit strange forbye. Folk said their hoose was full o books aboot Socialism. Hambo Jack's wife used to visit them before she had her first fall, and bring them sweets. Neighbours raised them, bringing meals in and giving their strange silent ways an understanding smile. "Shell shocked," they were. The oldest boy, caa'd Stanley too, died wae T.B. at the age o 21. He looked mair like a gangly 16. In fact, he collapsed crossing the Blackfort Road and was run over by a tram. For years after the tram driver used to visit the other boy, Eric. The mair Eric was in his late teens, he had a real conductor's ticket punch, and a tram driver's hat. He travelled free and unhindered with these, anywhere in Bigganreek. As an elderly, strange man, Eric would dash oot o his hoose in Samoa Street when he heard a car coming. Standing on the edge o the fitpad he would wave the motor past, as if he was a traffic policeman. Yinst the vehicle had passed, he would stand oot in the middle o the road wae his arm raised, stopping all the imaginary following traffic. Syne, on his way back into his hoose, he would wave the phantom cars on wae an impatient and stern gesture. Such a rigmarole Eric went through without regard to time o day, or even if he had company in his ain hoose.

It's no that Eric was completely daft, or even saft in the heid. Apart frae his dependency on others for the basics o life, and his quirky compulsive habits, he was fit to argue politics and religion. Ma Burke could hae been richt aboot Hambo Jack, up to a point. He never bullied Eric, and even sat in with him, alane, talking about Dear knows what. Hambo roared wae lauchter when Eric dashed oot to do his traffic control bit, and then returned as if he had just been bringing the milk in. Ma Burke said Hambo Jack sat and read books in Eric's. "Dead clever ye know, the pair o them. Far more learnin' in them than ye'd think," she said. But if Eric did talk sense about politics it was only to Hambo Jack. When he came into Ernie Gamble's it was only for feeding the pigeons. He came and went at that as often as he liked, taking a fistful o feed frae an enamel tin wae a lid, and feeding them yin grain at a time frae atween his thumb and forefingers. When Eric taen a notion o feeding the gutty-hoakers – the street pigeons – Ernie wanted to keep the pigeon food in the kitchen, but Iris said the vermin would come into the hoose. Sae an automatic food dispenser was constructed, but Eric still came wae crusts o bread to feed the pigeons. Only the roon crusts o a plain loaf he brocht. No the straight crusts frae the other end o the slice, for Eric ate those. Then Eric started feeding the gutty-hoakers on his ain window sill.

When he was aulder he didnae wear his tram driver's hat roon the streets onie mair. Kids teased him aboot it, the mair the adults would tell them off. Everybody protected Eric and had a soft spot for him. What else could they do when even Hambo Jack looked after him? Ma Burke said if Hambo Jack wasnae kind to Eric Bates, then naebody else would be. They only did it acause they were feared o Hambo.

The yin time he still wore the cap was when he followed the band. The Claw Defenders Flute Band was the band in question – it was the only one Eric took onie tent o. When setting off frae the band hall in the waste grun', or when returning frae a parade, Eric was there, in front. When passing a side street he would do his traffic-peeler-come-parade-marshal act, stopping encroaching traffic frae the side streets and waving the Claw Defenders past. Yinst the band had wheeled oot onto the Blackfort Road, however, Eric would turn back and march hame, whistling.

But all this came to an end when Eric died in his sleep in a chair by the fire. Mrs Hanna had fun' him the next morning, and run across the street to get Iris Gamble. Somebody had sent for a clergyman, wha was inside the house, and a clutch o shocked, whispering women were on the fitpad ootside when Hambo Jack arrived. The minister rushed oot when Hambo went berserk. He pulled the gas meter and its lead pipes clean off the walls wae yin hand. Oot through the window into the street it came, wae part o the lead pipes still attached like an umbilical cord. Hambo Jack appeared at the door and the women scattered. The minister walked awa as brisk as dignity would allow.

Police, Ambulance, Fire Brigade and men frae the Gas Department arrived. Half the street had to be cleared. If the gas went off it would be like a scene from the Blitz again. Yinst the gas leak frae a single lead pipe pulled oot o the wall had been stopped, and Eric Bates's corpse lifted frae the fitpad ootside into the ambulance and taen awa, all but the police were chased. The pursuers were a poking, shouting, pointing and pulling clutch of Samoa Street women. There was nae doot Eric had died o natural causes, but some said there had already been a gas leak afore Hambo arrived. But then they wanted to blame somebody and the Gas Department was guid eneuch. The hale event had taen on a bit o street theatre.

The tragedy o Eric's death had a dramatic impact on the Claw. The mair he was weel into his seventies, he was an innocent child. To maist he was like yin o their ain family, ignored by the outside world – the City Council, politicians, the churches and the moneyed bosses wha could hae made a difference if they'd only knowed aboot him. To Hambo Jack he had been not just ignored, but abused, by all them self-serving cleeks. Ken Gamble telt his father that Hambo Jack had really loved him. Even Ken was deeply disturbed by Eric's death.

"Ye what?" Ernie said, shocked by his son's strange choice of words – or did he mean something worse?

"I mean, like King Lear really loved his fool," Ken explained. "Ye know, Shakespeare an' that."

A dizzen o jokes ran through Ernie's heid, but he said naethin.

It was hard, even for Ken, to understand why Eric's death

had such an impact. Years later, but only then, could they see that it had symbolised the end o an era. The Claw was being redeveloped, if you looked at it in terms o biggins. It was being dispersed, if you saw it frae the people's viewpoint. Only an uneasy, instinctive reaction at the time sowed seeds o suspicion in maist folks' minds. They thocht that their scattering was being wrocht at by City planners wha had reached an understanding wae the churches, the politicians, and the civil servants. And what used to pass for industry.

"The Bates brothers was just cannon fodder, like their da," Hambo Jack told an attentive group of ears in the Friesian Bull. It wasnae so much a political analysis as a recognition that the last link had been severed between the Claw and thon black, black wastage o the Somme.

"An' the rest of us, an' all," Andy Murphy said. "D'ye want the ban' out for the funeral, Hambo?"

Hambo Jack straightened himsel up in his seat and glared at Andy. His piercing stab o a look sent a shock wave roon the pub table.

"He's just tryin' to help," pleaded yin o the company.

"Plaise yerself, Murphy," Hambo said through his teeth.

Andy Murphy and Billy Gamble was the only twa members o the Claw Defenders Band that had been at the death scene afore the polis arrived. They did turn oot for the funeral, the hale band, smart and bricht in their uniforms amang the drab colours of the rest o the crowd. It was frae oul ma Burke's hoose, and Samuel Agnew was in charge of the arrangements, after a fashion.

"Nobody wi' a dog-collar," Hambo had ordered. "Samuel Agnew can do the words."

Samuel and Alice Agnew lived simple and quiet at the end o Fiji Street wae their only daughter, Ruth. They were good living. Not churchy, but not quiet aboot religion either.

Samuel was a street corner preacher, a distributor o tracts, and avoided by all wha socht a quiet life and were able to save themsels. Everything, tae Samuel, was black or white, evil or Godly, and every shade o dairkness was called oot, and prayed agin, even oot in the street wi his Bible in upraised hand. The dairk side included maist o everybody else's everyday life in the Claw, but Hambo liked the way he black-mouthed clergymen and politicians the loudest. Ma Burke, nae saint hersel, had the same positive view o Samuel Agnew as she had o Hambo Jack. Sure if Sam wasnae a real man o principle, he would be a big clergyman living comfortably in Southcity.

The band formed a bare-headed double line on either side o the coffin. Their blue Glengowries wae white feather plumes were rolled up and tucked under their left oxters. A few veterans o the First World War, surviving comrades o Stanley Bates's, turned up wae overcoats and medals pinned on the ootside, and cried tears. It was yin o the biggest turnoots for a funeral the Claw had seen for years. The only face that wasnae glum was Samuel Agnew's, as he walked Bible in hand in front o the coffin. He micht'a been taen for the undertaker in his gleaming white collar and black tie and suit, except that he smiled and nodded at the lines o women on either fitpad. It was as if he was the prood father at his dauchter's wedding.

And sae the Claw said farewell to the last o the Bateses. Eric had nae relatives left, nane for the mourners to shake hands wae. All the more reason for the street to feel like a family. A press photographer had taen a photo, but naethin appeared in the papers. They had halted ootside Eric's hoose. The broken window glass had been brushed up, but the dark red gas meter still hung into the street wae a lead pipe attached. It was like a heart ripped oot o a breest, still hanging by an artery.

Andy Murphy and a few others frae the band came back to Eric's auld hoose the next day. Although it wasnae theirs, they boarded up the broken window anyway. A man frae the Gas Department had come back to take away the meter. He asked Andy who he was as he came through the house wae a hammer in his hand.

"Residents Association," he said, "makin' sure we don't get squatters."

Andy walked on oot to the back toilet in the back yard and broke the bottom o the pottery toilet bowl wae yin clash o the hammer. Another sharp strike on the cistern at head height and the cast iron cracked, letting oot a second flood o water. He walked back oot, silently, past the Gas man, leaving him to lock the front door.

The affection felt for poor Ernie throughout the Claw was transferred, in a sense, to his hoose. No because it was itsel a throw-back. There was nae love lost on the auld-farrent sticks o furniture, or the older, apen-top range. But it was a place o strang, and strange, associations. Whaever moved in would definitely hae to get it fixed up by the landlord first. It didnae even come up to health or cooncil standards, but Eric would never let anybody like that in to change it, never mind complain.

When the builders came, different neighbours would dander in and chat while they were working. Len Bones came and took away the remaining coal that was stacked loosely in the back corner o the yard. He also cleaned oot the few shovelfuls o coal kept handy under the stairs. The place was given a rough repair job rather than a refurbishing. The back yard had a clutter o scrap timber and other rubbish. The builder's rubbish was dumped oot there too. The next tenants could redd it oot themsels.

"Hey mister, any oul wood for the bonefire?" The pair o dirty-faced wee lads appeared in the back yard of Eric's auld hoose when Len Bones was rummaging aboot.

"Ay," he said, looking behind a wheen o planks stacked agin the wall, "take thon oul settee, and the rest o' them bits o' timber."

"Hey, lads." He cried them back after they were leaving wae the first load dragging ahint them. "A'll put the settee out in the street for ye an' ye can push it on the casters."

"Thanks mister."

Len Bones smiled. "D'ye know the coal-yard up the back o' Brackenridge Street?"

"Ay."

"Come up themorra an' get a pile o' oul doors an' things."

When the wood gatherers arrived at Bones's Coal Yard the next day, there was a lot mair nor the original twa. Aboot a dizzen boys and twa or three scruffy wee dolls. The bigger boys organised a chain to carry off their spoils in single file, like ants. After the last salvaged door and broken palette had been removed, Len called the twa original lads back.

Expectant, so they were, that mair generosity would flow. It had been a bit o an adventure anyway, getting in roon the back o the coal yard. Len walked ower til the piles o different grades o coal and slack. Some o them had buckets o white-wash thrown up the face o the pile.

"What's thon white for mister?"

"Well if anybody tries for to nyuck any in the night," Len explained. "Wait an' A'll show ye."

He walked ower to yin o the piles. Sticking oot frae under-neath, partly buried, was a lang iron pipe. It was thicker than a rainwater down-pipe, but aboot the same length. Len lifted the end o the pipe, levered it up and pulled the rest o it oot frae under the coal. As he did so, the face o the coal moved. The mini landslide left a black scar on the white-splattered face.

"See what happens, if anybody touches it?"

"We cud do that, mister, so we cud." Len watched as the two boys struggled to lift the iron pipe wae the intention o using it as a buttering ram on the other piles o coal.

"A tell ye what," Len said. "Cud yis do a wee job for me boys?"

"Ay, mister," they replied eagerly.

"Take that pipe down til the emp'y house yis were at yesterday, an' leave it in the yard. Up agin the back corner."

"An' then what?"

"A'll see yis down there in half an hour."

Off the wee lads ploitered, yin at each end o the iron pipe. Every twenty yards or so they clanked it doon for a rest and to change hands.

The pipe had been yin o a number under the coals in the coal yard. All part o a dry test run for Ernie Gamble's water-divining machine. Len was gye keen to help Ernie and keep an ee on progress.

Back at Eric Bates's auld hoose, Len went roon for to check the delivery. He riz the pipe up length ways, up agin the back corner o the yard. The top o the pipe stood higher nor the yard waa, in the back corner foment the entry, in the neuk frae where the last o Eric's coals had been redd oot. In fact, you could see the pipe sticking up frae the end o the back entry, for there was nae pigeon lofts doon that side.

For four weeks, Eric Bates's hoose stood empty afore there was any word o new tenants.

"Who's them new ones that's got Eric's house, Hambo?"

It was a Tuesday nicht, and Hambo Jack had turned up at a poorly attended band practice in the Claw Defenders F.B. hall. He sometimes wandered in when a tune was in full swing, stood at the back, lit a cigarette, and wandered back oot when the tune was finishing. This time he had stayed on. The question had been posed by a bruiser o a drummer.

"Just you stick to the drums, son, and never mind," Hambo answered in his low, gratey, monotone voice.

"I was just askin', so A was," the drummer replied.

"A said – just you mind your business and I'll mind mine – RIGHT?" Rarely had Hambo to raise his voice.

"Tom," Andy Murphy intervened, "just pay attention, up here. Right boys, two five-beat rolls an' the same again." Hambo Jack left, and the practice broke up after the tune was repeated. It had lost its punch, and the whole band felt put off by the visit.

It was no haeing been telt, and no kenning wha was moving in, that had Hambo Jack irritated. Not knowing meant they maun be ootsiders.

As the furniture and bits and pieces arrived, the neighbour women gathered roon the door. The youngish couple didnae seem uneasy wae the attention, so they got a friendly reception. There was nae jooking frae behind curtains in Samoa Street. The neighbours went straight in there wae, "D'yis want a han', love?"

"Lovely lukin' couple, so they are," yae woman said loudly to the rest, weel within earshot o the lovely couple.

"An' are ye from round here, love?" another asked directly.

"Just up the Blackfort Road, Jacob Street. M'da's Andrew Graham, ye know, on the Council."

Well, that seemed aa richt then. Annie's new husband was no frae Bigganreek but his name was Paul Kavanagh and he came frae County Cavan. He had a brother living over off the Mossvale Road. The neighbours didnae find that oot until weeks after. It didnae matter to maist. Well, no for the time being. "We'll take them as we find them," they said. But Paul was on a sort o probation.

Even Len Bones was friendly enough. "I'll drap ye aff two

bags of coal themorra, free like, just to start yis aff."

The coal was duly delivered. Len dumped it in the corner, burying the base o an iron pipe – the yin the weans delivered a wheen o days back.

"Thon oul pipe's mine: A'll come an' get it soon."

"We'll need a proper coal bunker built here," Annie said to Paul when Len was emptying the coal. "The muck'll be all over the yard intil the house."

"I'll get that done for ye too," Len said. "Just leave it with me." If they had known ocht aboot Len Bones they would hae been gye an suspicious o his helpfulness. As for the muckle great pipe left sticking oot o the coals, it was tae prove mair than an intrusion.

Joe Stitt was waiting at the time clocks o Wetherals on Monday morning. When Jack M'Clean had punched his new week's card in, he put it back against his number on the wall rack. But Joe Stitt's nicotine-stained fingers lifted it oot again just as soon. He seemed to be inspecting it as he spoke.

"Were ye at the big match on Saturday?"

It would have been a bigger topic of conversation if Jack had missed it, for City had been playing the other half o the Bigganreek auld firm – Mossvale. City drew as much o their support frae the Blackfort Road as frae the Brickworks district, where the "Holy City" ground was. Mossvale's support, naturally eneuch, was frae the streets off the Mossvale Road.

It micht hae been a sort o a test o Jack's loyalty; and he reacted indignantly. "Ay, A was – an' yerself?"

Joe Stitt ignored the question. "Thon was a good chance there that ye missed."

Jack was puzzled. "What was that?"

"A toul ye A could get you an Lily a house in the Claw, so A did. Well, ye're too late, for it's took."

Jack went on into work with his usual Monday-morning feeling. Lily had told him all aboot her brother attending to Eric Bates's funeral. She had hinted aboot the hoose, he thocht. But he didnae think she meant for the twa o them.

"Billie Jack!"

It was Lily's brother, Billy. "Ye at the match on Saturday?"

"That's twice A've been ast that in as many minutes. O' course A wus."

Billy smiled at Jack's ill temper.

"Ye don't luk that plaised wae another magnificent victory for the British Empire."

The Mossvale supporters were thocht o as aliens. The Mossvale Road wasnae just a different religion, if a road can hae a religion.

"Sure wasn't A back at your house after?" Jack added.

It was like a sleeping giant, the Mossvale Road. And you never thocht o it as haeing real people, till you saw the feck o them at the other end o the fitbaa grun. Jack wasnae sure aboot the singing and all yinst he seen the reaction. "Let sleepin' dogs lie," was what Ernie had to say about such coat-trailing. But yin man's civil richts was the tither man's coat-trailing, and the hale o Bigganreek would pay the price o that some day.

Chapter 4

Quality Control

Joe Stitt was curious about Jack M'Clean's promotion. Suspicious, maybe, micht hae been a better description. "What do you know about food quality?" he asked aboot a fortnicht after Jack got his move to Quality Control.

"Nathin'. A'm not even workin' wi' the food anyhow."

"What has he got ye doin' then? Washin' the Wetherals' big cars?"

"Mr Colin nor none o' the Wetherals comes in the food lab," Jack said defensively. "A just check the seal on the tin cans – ye know wi' pliers an' a screw gauge an' that." He thocht that his work, involving the metal cans and men's tools wasnae as cissy-sounding as checking the quality o the food. Joe Stitt didnae think so. He snortit derisively, turned away, and then came back again.

"An' did he ast ye anythin' about me?"

Jack was puzzled and shook his heid convincingly. For the next wheen o days, Jack thocht on what micht hae got Joe Stitt's heid so fashed wae Mr Colin. He couldnae mind any time Mr Colin had made mention o Joe Stitt. But he had speired Jack aboot this fella that had got shot outside the factory. Mr Colin seemed relieved that it was something to do wae the fitbaa match.

"You might expect that sort of thing in the back streets of the Blackfort Road, but not on the steps of our factory," quo he. At that point Jack bit his lip. He would aye be scum himsel, in the Wetherals' een. He realised then that he detested Mr Colin even more than the worst o the hard men o the Claw. Hooaniver, it gien him a smile to think on the scare Mr Colin had gotten. Maybe he thocht it was an assassination attempt on his ain sel? He was big-heidit eneuch, so he was.

Back at Lily's hoose twathree nichts later, Ernie was the first to show a real interest in Jack's new job. Lily's father wasnae satisfied till Jack had every detail described o how he took a tin can frae the packing line.

"The lid comes separate, ye see, an' this machine scoots roun' the outside o' each tin an' laps the edges roun' each other, an wee rollers squeezes the rim tight."

"An' there's no glue nor solderin'?"

"Na, an' she's well sealed, for there's pressure builds up in the tin cans as well as not havin' leaks."

Jack had to apen ilka tin wae a rotary tin-opener. Then he had to make a cut through the rim, where the remains o the lid had been folded and rolled into the can side. That was the way the sealed rim was formed. Jack tried to show it by folding two edges o the tablecloth thegither. Wae a strang pull, the hale strip o the can-lid seal came oot.

Ernie wanted to know if Jack wrocht the machine that put the lids on the food cans.

"No, no. A just check that the lids is well sealed – not them all, just the one, every hour, aff the line."

"Houl' on," Ernie said as he gaed oot tae the working kitchen. He had to see this for himsel, so he took down a tin o beans, and apened the lid wae an ordinary, lever opener which gave a very ragged edge. The beans were put in a small cooking pot and stuck back on the shelf.

"Da, what are you doin'?" Lily shouted out, bored stiff with all the talk about work. "Whenever mammie comes in yous'll be for it."

"I'm just gettin' a tin, to see what way this seal works," Ernie replied, washing oot the can under the tap.

"Right," he said, coming back into the parlour where Lily and Jack were sitting. He had a pair of pliers and wire cutters in yin hand and the dripping wet can in the other.

Jack took them and demonstrated his newly learnt skill. Ernie took the nine-inch curling length of metal strip and examined it closely.

"Ye see the way the two bits overlaps there? A have to put a micrometer screw gauge on and measure the overlap, an' write the measurement down in a sheet, every hour."

Ernie wasnae interested in that side o things, just on how the dry seal worked. "It's a wonder," he said, "the' never done this on ships, for it gives a great seal."

Lily was delighted when she heard her mum at the door. Ernie got up quickly, taking the can and pieces back oot. "Ye see Lily, ye shud a'ways luk at the way things is done. There's no such a thing as a new idea. Ye just take one idea an' use it on somethin' else."

"Ach, Jack, you're here, what about ye? I'm wrecked, so I am." As Iris dropped down exhausted, Ernie came back from the working kitchen.

"I'm starvin'. I've just put some beans on when I heard ye comin' in the door."

"Beans!" Iris said, surprised. "You? What's got into ye?"

"Good for the brain cells, so they are," Ernie said and winked at Jack.

Iris was more surprised that Ernie had put a pot full o beans on the gas ring than she was that he wanted fed.

"See him," she said to Jack, "he cud'n get himself a drink o' milk if the tap was'n aff the bottle."

Lily was more interested in this conversation. "How come da works all day out in the shed, an' the minute he comes in the workin' kitchen, he's han'less?"

Ernie just grinned as the women ganged up on him. Jack had become the unofficial judge and jury as Iris continued her evidence of how useless her man was in the kitchen.

"Did you ever make yer own piece for work, Jack?"

"Well, at school …"

Without waiting for an answer, Iris continued: "Whenever our Lily was bad wi' the whoopin' cough this time, an' I was runnin' roun' in circles, I ast him to do his own piece for work. 'The butter's too hard,' he sez. Four bits o' good bread he had torn to pieces, crumbs all over the place. So he puts the butter on the stove an' melts it an pours it over the bread. Useless, so he is. Couldn't do an egg if it was boiled for him first."

"I used to do all that when I was a wee lad," Ernie said.

"First I heard of it," Iris said with her arms folded, hovering between irritation and good humour.

"Oh, ay, I did. When I was a wee lad A cum home from the Tuesday night Gospel meetin' saved – ay, me, saved – an' I toul my da, an' he sez, 'Good, ye can get in more coal for the fire, an' make us all a cup o' tay'. I was a fortnight runnin' messages, an' butterin' digestive biscuits before I wised up."

"Ye shudn't joke about things like that," Iris said crossly. Lily thought about the connection between religion and the kitchen – baith of them the woman's concern. But she said nothing.

"Anyway, the top chefs is all men," Ernie said.

"Not roun' here they're not. Jack, son, cud ye ate some beans?"

"No thanks, Mrs Gamble, I'm a' right."

Jackson, the stores foreman in Wetherals, had told his ain boss that he didnae want to lose Jack to the Quality Control section. But Mr Colin had big ideas for Jack. Or so he said.

"In an' out wi' ye all the time, I suppose?" Joe Stitt was still curious aboot Colin Wetheral's intentions.

"No, he was at the start, but he wud be roun' talkin' to Lily more than to me," Jack replied.

"A toul' ye about the house," Joe Stitt continued. "Just watch it wi' him – an' let me know if he goes on to Lily about it."

"Lily sez she wudn't want to live roun' here, anyhow."

"I cud'a had a good handy wee house for yis in Samoa Street, but it's too late now," Joe said as he ground oot his cigarette butt on the concrete floor o the staff canteen. He stood up and, walking off, added, "Min' now. Anytime." Half way across the yard between the canteen and the factory loading bay, Joe Stitt stopped suddenly, turned and walked back to Jack.

"Is Wetheral lukin' for ye to go on day-release or night Tech or anything?"

"Na."

"Or to move ye roun' the factory for to learn all the jobs?"

"No – well he did say that if I did all right in Quality he might give me a spell in the Dispatch Office. Lily says he might even give her a go in the office."

"You just watch him," Joe said and walked away again.

Lily seemed moody on the bus hame. She didnae want Jack to walk her doon the street. Afore Jack could get up from his seat, she said, "Sure I'll see you in the morn," and aff she went. He returned her stilted smile and half-hearted wave frae the bus window.

Lily had a lot on her mind. Mr Colin was guid-look-ing. College-boy, sort-of-film-star lang fair hair he had, weel brushed back in a single wave. No yin drop of brylcream, but.

"Did Jack tell you about what we could do for you? The house or whatever?" Mr Colin's question had taken her by surprise. She had pretended not to know anything about it.

"I told him we could," he continued, "we'd be very keen to – to let you have one of the firm's houses. Once you were married, of course, and rent-free if you both kept on working here."

"Oh Jack and me's not talked about gettin' married or nothing like that, Mr Colin."

"You're not that serious then?"

"Well, no, but he's not bringing it up."

He flashed a warm smile at Lily. What perfect teeth, she thocht. It maun be the guid breeding or something.

"He must be a fool then, Lily, a lovely-looking girl like you." He smiled again as he walked off, charmed by her blush.

"Oooh!" chorused Lily's mates as soon as he turned the corner. Lily blushed again and lauched. "Youse are just jealous," she said and carried on wae her job as if nothing exceptional had occurred. Pleased as punch she was but, and couldnae get it off her mind.

"Are ye in thenight?" Lily asked Ruth Agnew from Fiji Street. Ruth was a very close friend of Lily's, the mair she wouldnae mix with anybody other than Lily in Wetheral's. She had her father Samuel's religion and her mother Alice's homely gift of offering close sympathetic friendship on a just-when-needed basis. The religious isolation meant that she could be trusted not to spread gossip or break confidences. Whiles, Jack and Lily had visited the Agnews at Ruth's invitation. Ruth had openly told Lily that she had a notion o Jack herself, but Lily knew there was nae risk ava there.

"What do ye go round there for?" Jack had asked Lily at the beginning.

"We talk about stuff, just. She's man-mad ye know."

"Ruth? Sure she's never even been out wi' a boy."

"Doesn't stop her gettin' ideas. She's just waitin for God to send Mr Right round to the house some day."

When Lily got to Ruth's, she teemed oot her doubts. Nae mention was made o Mr Colin, the mair Ruth had witnessed them clicking.

"See Jack, well he's all right so he is, but —."

"But what?"

"A dunno. Maybe it's just me. How do ye know when ye're really in love, Ruth? Wud ye never wonder or have second thoughts?"

"Don't worry, Lily, when you meet the right man, you'll know all right." Ruth spoke wae, and frae, conviction, but no frae experience.

"Does that mean Jack doesn't be the right one, if A'm not sure? Like A'm atttractit to him an' all, an' he's a good, steady fella. Sometimes I think he's just too steady, but."

"Does he make you laugh?"

"Sometimes. He wud be serious more. Maybe he's too serious?"

"Well," Ruth said, "a man can't be too steady. If he's too serious, that's in your head. I mean, he can only be more serious than you want him to be."

Lily knowed that Ruth was richt. But she liked Jack, and so did her dad and the rest o the family. Maybe she was just going through a phase. She could tell that boys fun' her attractive, for she saw them looking at her – no her body, but her face. Billy's friends, Ken's friends, like Rabbie, and even Mr Colin. They often did nowadays, not like years ago when she was still at school.

Jack had nae sense o problems afoot, but he kent something was different. He thocht that Lily micht be getting bored wae the routine o their dates. But he liked the security o a routine, and they only went to the pictures when Lily wanted to, and they only watched the pictures Lily wanted to see, and they only called in to somebody's hoose for a visit when Lily wanted to, and they only visited Lily's friends, not his.

Wherever they went, Jack liked to get back to Lily's after and sit and hae a guid crack wae Ernie or Lily's brothers. It meant that Lily was never late in, no like Billy or Ken. There wasnae much opportunity for passion in all this, mair than could be snatched at the pictures or in shop doorways on the road hame.

Wednesdays, Fridays and Saturday nichts. That's when Jack took Lily oot. Thursday nicht was music nicht at Cherryhill Silver. In some ways Jack looked forward to the band practice on Thursday nichts mair than the weekends.

"Cud ye not miss thon oul ban' for one night?" Lily would demand when there was something she wanted to do on a Thursday.

"It's not like a melody flute ban', ye know," Jack explained. "There's parts an' all. If there's one bit missin', ye let the whole ban' down."

Lily's twa brithers had both been in The Claw Defenders years back, when they were wee. Ken had left when he went to College, but Billy was still there. The idea o joining Cherryhill Silver passed Ken's mind for a while. That was serious music, contests, music with different movements, composed special-like, rousing marches called "concert marches" that were even more rousing than the bang-bang tunes. Classical music wae dynamics. Ken went to a practice wae Jack yinst or twice to try it oot but he thocht they didnae take it seriously eneuch. Jack played bass trombone, alang wae three other ordinary trombones in that section. For practices, the sections sat roon three sides o a square, wae Walter Dibber and his conductor's music stand on the other. The trombones were in a row to Walter's richt, ahint the baritones and euphoniums. Ken was allowed to sit alangside Jack to try and follow the music. But the Bass trombone was the only instrument to be scored in the Bass Clef – no even the basses were. "Upside down music," Jack called it, "but easy enough when ye get the hang o' it."

So instead Ken followed the ordinary treble clef music o Ben Brown to his left. Oul Ben was baldy-heided and had a whistling hearing aid that he switched off every time the band struck up.

"What's that?" Ben said as Walter stopped a piece to complain aboot the overblowing.

"Can you not see?" Walter had said, poking his conductor's score with his white baton. "Double Ps is double Piano – twice as saft. Twice."

"Eh?" Ben whispered to Jack.

"He says belt it out," Jack whispered back and winked at Ken. But Ken couldn't resist pointing to the double piano sign on Ben's music and signalling a lowering motion with his hand.

"C'mon, c'mon, c'mon," Walter shouted impatiently, bringing his baton down from the poised position and rapping it on the top o the music stand. One discipline Walter always insisted on was that all instruments would be raised to mouths when he raised his baton.

In a small band hall the massive soond o a double-forte brass harmony was an exhilarating musical experience. The glory o the big chord was what brocht the maist o these men thegither week in, week oot. Like the triple-Amen frae a male voice choir, they needed the climax o a big brassy chord to round the nicht off.

Ken was brave and keen at the start. "Walter's right when he says the secret of good music is just good tuning."

"Ay, it just takes one learner out of tune and the whole ban' sounds crap," Jack agreed. "An' ye fair miss the drums."

But Ken still thought they didn't take it seriously enough. It was a shame, for some o the players were serious good musicians. And they could get a good sound on contest pieces.

"Dynamics, dynamics, luk at the dynamics," Walter would shout, putting his baton down on the ledge o his stand to stop the band.

"Staccato, staccato – short, sharp. I want it bouncy. Imagine you're an empty coke tin comin' down the lough on a choppy bit of water."

"Eh?" said Ben, fiddling at his ear.

"Staccato, short, sharp, crispy. I want potato crisps and yis're givin' me soda farls."

"What's he say?" Ben whispered again.

"I think he's wantin' a break. Crisps and lemonade, like," Jack said, and lauched. Ben cackled too.

Ken didnae stick wae it, and after a week or twa quit coming. Jack loved it, but it was more than the music. He had lang growed attached to the others, and even had an affection for the atmosphere o the band hall itsel. An auld fashioned gas meter on top o the music cupboard was the size o a large water-tank. It was the biggest Jack had ever seen – probably fit for a museum.

There was a loyalty in their comradeship. To lea' the band was all richt, but to leave it to join another band was regarded as treason.

When Lily started getting a bit funny wae Jack, he thocht quite a lot aboot leaving the band. He toyed wae the idea o joining Billy in The Claw Defenders – but no for lang. It wouldnae be ocht to do wae music, but it would certainly stitch himsel well and truly into Lily's circle. It was the glamour o the marching bands, the uniforms, and the bravado o this Mutual Protection Society that had taen him into Cherryhill Silver in the first place – not the music. But that was when he was ower young to realise that all bands wurnae the same. He started on the drums, and used to take his drumsticks to school tucked into his trouser belt, under his jacket. Paradiddles and rolls could be practised anywhere, but ceramic wash hand basins were guid. In fact, Jack had been learnt the rudiments o music frae a book propped apen behind the taps, drumming on the wash basin in the toilets o the band hall. He didnae show any interest in an instrument for years.

"Did you ever think of joinin' a band?" Jack speired at Lily yin nicht walking back doon the Blackfort Road frae the pictures.

"D'ye not think I'm a bit oul for paradin' in a wee tartan miniskirt an' an accordion?"

"There's plenty o' girls in brass bands now, ye know."

"Catch yerself on, Jack."

They stopped in the recessed doorway o a clothing shop, twa streets up frae the Friesian Bull, and close to the turn into Samoa Street. It was a dark, wet and windy nicht and the shelter was welcome. They often stopped there, a parting place, to say and kiss guidnicht. The window displays in the shop looked nae mair exciting at nicht, wae lighting and colour, than they did during the day. The dummies and clothes were drab. The owners were friends o the Agnews, and only sold respectable, Christian clothes.

Jack had been looking forward to their stop in the shop doorway. The picture hoose on this occasion was packed, and the folk there wanted to watch the picture, no jook roon courting couples. When Jack had started to wrap himself roon Lily, an oul wifie behind said loudly to her husband, "There's them aff agane. There's a time an' a place for everything. It's ridicilous." Jack looked roon and sat squarely back in his place. It was the same auld couple that had loudly complained yinst afore, months back. "Wud ye luk at them pair. He's in her sate an' she's in his. Ridicilous."

So the doorway became another ground for Jack's insecurity.

"D'ye think I'll en' up wi' a boss's job in Wetherals?" Jack asked. Lily looked slightly cool and uninterested. Not like she should if she was thinking about their future thegither.

"I dunno. Don't be tryin to be somethin' ye're not, like what our Ken does."

Lily looked particularly attractive in the dim licht. Her overcoat was apen wae the ends of a loose belt hanging doon, casual-like. She lent wae yin shoodher agin the side o yin o the windows. Baith hands were in her coat pockets. Jack turned towards her and slipped his hand inside her coat. As they engaged eyes, he went to kiss her. He needed the reassuring responses rather than the actual physical thing.

Lily never played games wae Jack, and she didnae stop his hand as it slid underneath her apen cardigan, ower her blouse and roon the back o her rib-cage. It was what she did that Jack was overly sensitive to. Her lips were soft, nice, but no pursed in response to his. She kept yin hand in her pocket, and the other on the back o his elbow. It was a twa-handed embrace he wanted, but what he got was as dead as the dummy in the shop window.

"Anything wrong?" he asked, pulling back into a casual mode to match hers.

"Na, I'm just thinkin'."

"What about?"

"Nathin'. Just …"

"Just what? C'mon …"

"It's all right, Jack. I'm just fed up wi' work. I better get on in."

"See ye themorra then?"

"Ay, right-oh. S'long, Jack." And she gien him a hairt-sinking half-hairtit smile as she went off without a good-night peck.

The drizzle-packed wind was blowing coldly into his face, as Jack strode up the Blackfort Road. Walking quick, and the cold sting in his face, he didnae dwell on things. Yinst he turned into the shelter o Champion Street, his mind jolted disturbingly back to Lily's mood. He hoped it was just a mood. He scanned his mind for what it was she had said or done that disturbed him the maist.

"I might be gettin a move in work, maself." He was pleased when she said it, at the time. But it was annoying him now. "Til the Dispatch Office. Mr Colin thinks I should get a try in the office."

"And Lily had the cheek to talk about me gettin' above maself," he thocht.

It wasnae late, but maist o the downstairs windows in Champion Street showed nae licht. No sae wae his ain hoose. He could see his mother sitting at the fire, dozing, as he passed his own window. In through the door he slid, bringing the key in oot o the lock as he came. By the time he walked the twathree steps into the kitchen parlour, his mother was up, slapping random flat surfaces wae a rag duster.

"You not in yer bed yet, ma?"

"A'm just done wi' yer clane shirt for themorra, an' yer da's shoes, an' … A think that's it now." She squared hersel up and looked at him as if she'd just fun' time frae her routine to notice him.

"Ye're drowndit. What did ye not put yer da's raincoat on for, like A toul ye? Were ye down the Road again thenight? A hope ye kept til the Main Road. A just don't like ye down them streets. If ye want to get on in Wetheral's ye'd better buck up yer ideas m'lad."

"There's nathin' wrong wi' the Claw, or the folks that live here," Jack said as he went up the stairs.

"A niver said there was," Mrs M'Clean said.

"Well not in the last five minutes, so ye never," Jack said back frae the top o the stairs.

"Wud ye houl yer whisht or ye'll wake yer da," Bessie M'Clean bellowed up the stairs.

Lily had left Jack to walk hame by hersel. It was only twa junctions doon the road, and then the length o Samoa Street. The wind and rain was on her back, pushing her coat ticht, but she could feel the cold and rain on the backs o her stockinged calves. She kept the collar o her coat turned up, to shelter her neck, and thocht aboot Jack's kiss. It was after-wards that she liked to think aboot the kissing. Before and after, thinking about it, was what she liked best. Whiles, she felt as if she enjoyed thinking aboot Jack, and talking aboot him to others, more than actually being wae him. Did that mean ocht in itsel? "Ae fand kiss, an' then we pairtit." The line o thon sang came into her mind. There was nae fand kiss thenicht at the parting place.

When Lily got hame, Ken and Billy were baith in. Ernie and Iris were away to their bed.

"Well, did ye tell him?" Ken asked, looking up frae the books on the table he was working wae and putting the end o his pen in his mooth.

"Tell who, what?" Lily said, shaking the wet off her coat and setting it ower the back o yin o the empty chairs at the table. Without waiting for the answer she already knew, she went oot into the working kitchen and filled the kettle.

"Tay, Billy?"

"Na."

"Ken?"

"Na. Did ye tell Jack – about you moving to the office job?"

Billy wriggled in his seat at the fire. He was stretched full oot wae his hands in his pockets staring into the coals.

"Sort of," Lily replied as casually as possible. "I mean, yes, but not that I'm movin' themorra."

Billy looked up at her, making Lily feel guilty and uncomfortable.

The next morning Lily explained to Jack on the bus why she was wearing her guid claes to work.

"Sure A toul ye last night. I don't think I'll like it, away from all the girls an' all. I don't have to move if I don't like it, so I don't."

"Ye niver said ye were movin' theday," Jack said ruefully.

"Sure you niver told me when you were movin' to Quality Control, before-han', like."

Lily was excited by the prospect, but nervous too, and annoyed at having to pretend she couldnae care less.

Yin forenoon, Jack was on his road up the office wae a full clip-boord o these quality check sheets he aye had to leave in afore dinner time. The glass screens let him catch a glimpse o Lily in her new office. It was real freedom, being able to walk roon the factory during working hours, mair or less at will, sae lang as he aye looked busy. He managed that by walking quick, carrying papers or something in his hand. He seen Lily laughing and talking wae her hands waving aboot her to the twa other women in her office. She had it gye and easy now too. But then he saw it. What a scunner. Colin Wetheral, wae his wavy, fair, bloody hair, sitting on the end o Lily's desk, smiling, cracking jokes. His leg was in a plaster. Pity it wasnae his neck, thocht Jack. He was definitely chatting Liz up – wasn't he? – Jack kept asking himsel.

Come dinner time, there was nae avoiding the argument.

"An' how come he got his leg bust then?"

"On holiday. He was water-skiing, ye know, just learnin'."

"Slap it up him, serves him right."

"What's wrang wi' you? Can he not go on holiday an' enjoy himself then?"

Jack had a mind to gie Lily the bit about the big nobs being wasters, getting their money for foreign holidays frae speeling ower honest folk's backs.

But he knew Lily would lauch at him. He could hear her saying, "honest folk? – like you an' Joe Stitt an' all?" And maybe she would quite like the fantasy o being yin o his slaves.

"All that's not for the likes o' us," quo he, weakly.

"An' why shouldn't it be?" Lily retorted. "If ye must know, Colin said I would have really enjoyed it."

"Oh it's Colin now is it? An ye talk about me getting notions."

Lily would be naebody's slave, but truth was she was starting to hae day-dreams about her and Colin – or rather her and big cars and big hooses wae kitchens the size o her ain hoose, and strutting to church wae big hats, and struttin' aboot at parties wae bricht dresses, and coloured drinks, and fancy claes, and presents o new jewellery gien as a surprise afore gaun oot tae the theatre – an aaboadie talking proper. Oh ay, there micht be problems, but Colin could see she was as guid as onie o them.

The dreams aye turned a bit soor whenever she thocht o Colin leaving her hame some nicht, maybe after a date, to Samoa Street – no that she would hae onie problems flitting frae there – but her brothers, and her ma, and her da's inventions? She felt perfectly ashamed that, for yin wee minute, she had felt ashamed o them.

"Lily," the girls in the office said that afternoon, "I think Mr Colin fancies you."

"Catch yerself on." Lily blushed as she answered.

"What wud ye do if he ast ye out?" Mavis continued.

"There's no way. Anyhow, A have a boy. Why? D'ye know if he has gone out wi' any other girls in the factory?"

"Ooo–ee–ooo!" the other girls lauched and chorused as Lily blushed again.

Jack sensed it all. Quality control? Damned right.

Chapter 5

Lifts

Ye wouldnae hae knowed Eric Bates's auld hoose whenever the Kavanaghs moved in. Annie had Paul painting and decorating and in and oot the shops getting wallpaper picked.

"Are you colour-blind?" she would say after inviting him to pick what wallpaper he liked the best. But she aye gien him the final choice o whatever she had it narrowed doon tae. Always. Nae matter how lang it took him to pick the richt yin.

They had got married in the Parish Church further up the Blackfort Road, and stopped wae her folks till the hoose was got ready. Nane o Paul's family had come to the wedding, nane ava. But that was another story for there was soorness aboot it.

"Paul?" Annie cried at him frae their new bathroom wae its ceramic wash-hand basin (the only coloured yin in the street).

Paul was just back in after his first day at work after their flitting. He was an apprentice electrician wae a lift installation company, a start Annie's father had got him. It was hard to get taen on as a prentice to onie trade, but Cooncillor Agnew boasted he had a few "electrical connections."

"What's the matter?" Paul cried back.

"Were you up in the bathroom?"

"Ay," he replied, wondering what was up.

"Ye've left the soap in the basin, after I had the whole place cleaned."

"Catch yerself on," Paul shouted wae an irritated sound in his voice. "Can A not wash ma hands in my own house when A come back from ma day's work?"

Annie came in to the room, a wee bit chastened, but glowing with house pride in her man.

"A've yer tay ready for ye pet," she smiled.

There were a few bits and pieces needit done, and yin o the twa bedrooms wasnae touched yet. All the same, it was guid for the twa o them just tae sit in their new hoose at nicht, planning mair.

"Ye would hardly credit it, this parlour," Paul said as he sat looking round the room. "When ye think o' what it was like before."

They wouldnae hae gas in the house, just electric. The electric cooker in the back working kitchen was rented, but near everything else was new. In fact, the working kitchen itself was sort o new. There had been a scullery and an auld jaw box o a sink, but the only cooker in the Bates's time had been the open-grate range in the front room.

During the renovation a van came wae three men and a curator frae the museum. Apart frae a wheen o notes and photos, the range was the only thing they wantit. Noo a wee modern Devon grate sat where the range had been, and the kitchen parlour was just a parlour.

A while after the renovations, Paul fun' some twathree books, a diary and a box o papers up in the attic. He thocht the man frae the museum micht hae an interest so he gien them a ring frae his work the next morning. But they wurnae interestit ava. Neither was Annie. She wouldnae let him keep onie o the auld gas lichts nor onie other bits and pieces o Eric

Bates's either. If the museum thocht that only the range was worth keeping, sure they were the experts. And it wasnae as if Eric Bates was famous or ocht. Mind, the mair it was the Kavanagh's new hoose now, for years after it still got called Bates's auld hoose.

The very first proper visitors Annie and Paul had into their hoose was Lily and Jack. They just called in on them after the pictures yin nicht. Well, Annie had told Lily they could any time. It was a polite evening supper they had. Annie got out her good china plates and made triangular pan loaf sandwiches wae the crusts cut aff, and a tray o taypots and saucers and cups and spoons and sugar dish and matching milk jug. They talked polite too, but it was maistly Annie done the talking.

"This man tried to walk out o' the pictures thenight," Lily had said the minute they arrived, "when the Queen was playin'. An' there was near a fight, for a gang o' lads run out to the back an' stood in his road."

"The're all as bad as one another," Paul said.

Lily blushed when she minded the company was sort o mixed. Paul smiled, understanding her embarassment. "An' the're just the same down south."

Frae that point, Annie had free range o' the conversation.

"And your Ken's at College, isn't he?" Annie speired. It was the first time she had talked aboot ocht other than hersel, her Paul, her da or her hoose. By rights it would hae been polite conversation, asking after others, but wae Annie it was just nebby-neighbouring – or at best she was looking for bits o information that micht raise the tone o the street.

"Yes, this two years, so he is."

"And what's he reading?"

"Reading? A couldn't say. He's a'ways reading."

"A mean, what subjects is he taking at college?"

"Oh, I thought …," Lily started before she took the giggles and forgat to gie an answer.

On other nichts, Jack and Lily would arrive, mair as guests o Paul's than Annie's. If Annie wasnae the host, she would stay most o the nicht in the working kitchen, but nae sandwiches would appear. Whiles, Jack would call roon his lane, or wae some other billie alang wae him.

"Ye comin' out, Paul?" It was a bit like "Ye comin' out to play?"

"Na," he said, looking ower his shoodher; "c'mon in but."

It never was yin o thae hooses the neighbours just walked in and oot o. Len Bones was hardly let in the yard door to deliver the coal. Annie wouldnae speak to him ava, and when Paul come hame frae work she would say, "An' when are ye goin' to get the coalman to take thon oul pipe away from our back yard?"

And Annie never bothered much with her neighbours either. No that she wasnae friendly. If she was walking up the street she would beam and say hello to anybody stood in their doorways. It's just that she had no interest in crossing other folk's thresholds. O coorse, gye and often she had to go looking for Paul at neighbours' doors.

"Is our Paul here?" she would say.

"Ay, c'mon in love!"

Yin sic day it was Iris Gamble. Annie thocht the Gambles were better than the rest in Samoa Street – mair like hersel.

"No, thanks, it's just his tea's ready, so it is." And back hame she would walk.

"Ye're wantin' for yer tay Paul," said Iris, back in the parlour where he was sitting lounged out mair comfortable than he would sit at hame. Jack and Lily were both there too, talking about their new jobs at Wetherals. Annie would hae been impressed wae Lily and her office job, and Jack in Quality

Control. Not that Annie worked hersel, noo that she was married. She stood out that way too, for maist o the young women folk in the Claw worked part-time at something. Mair o them had jobs nor the men. And Annie would parade up the street to the shops, dressed to the nines in the middle o the day, and in the middle o the week. But she still smiled and was friendly to folks. Naebody would call her "stuck up" if she could help it.

Ernie wasnae interestit in Lily's new job in the office.

"And is the lift doors on a 'lectric circuit?" he asked Paul, "so as it can't budge till the outside gate and the lift gate is shut?"

"It's all new automatic doors, now." Paul said, "Works wi' a button."

"Ye mean a motor?"

"Ay," Paul replied, getting up to go. He mistook Ernie's interest in lifts for an interest in himsel. He liked the Gambles – nice folk. Ernie was left wondering how the doors on the lift and the outside doors on different floors could all work on the same motor.

"C'mon in an' see us any time, son," Ernie cried after him.

"See ye, Paul."

"See ye, Jack, cheerio now, Miss Gamble, Lily."

Whenever he was away, Iris broke the lang silence, thinking aloud.

"I don't see why everybody brings religion intil it. A don't care what sort he is, he's a nice fella, him, so he is."

"A hear ye were roun' in thon new house in Samoa Street wi' Lily the other night." Joe Stitt never was one to waste Ulidican's time wae idle crack.

"Ay?" Jack answered.

"A toul ye A cud'a had it for you and Lily, but maybe it's

even better now it's all done up?"

"The' have it brave an nice, so the' do." Usually, Jack never fashed his heid aboot what Joe Stitt was playing at. But this time he cocked his lugs.

"A'm not takin' any house from Wetherals, if that's what's aitin ye," quo he. "Anyhow, A don't think Mr Colin's offer still houls."

"You an' Lily still getting on a' right?" Joe speired, catching the reek o an unaisy hairt. "Mr Colin's roun' in Lily's office a desperate lot."

Jack walked off, scunnered. If Joe Stitt could see it, then it was richt.

"Never mind him, we can sort him out easy enough," he called after Jack as he disappeared through the double swing doors onto the main stairs.

Colin Wetheral was a bit fed up getting. He had got Jack M'Clean a promotion, and little thanks for it. It was easy to see that Jack was hostile to him.

"Is M'Clean all right, Joe? What do you think?" he speired at Joe Stitt yin forenoon.

"What d'ye mean, Mr Colin? Honest like?" Joe Stitt aye talk't up tae Colin Wetheral, wha had perfect trust in him. And Joe aye let him think he was like a faithfu retainer. In a way he was, for his grannie cleaned for the Wetherals for years after their big new hoose in Cherryhill was biggit. Colin had known Joe Stitt to see frae they were baith wee fellas. And Joe had made a career oot o being well-in wae the Wetherals.

"I'm sure he's honest enough, but I get the feeling he would knife me in the back, given half a chance."

"Ay, Mr Colin, he's worth a-watchin'. He cud be sleek-it enough. D'ye want me to keep an eye on him, an' ask around?"

"Would you, Joe? Thanks very much. I wouldn't like any

accidents to happen. Do you think he might be mixed up, you know, involved, with any bad elements?"

"A wudn't know, Mr Colin, but A cud try an' find out."

Colin Wetheral's father, auld Mr Colin, was retired frae his job as Ulidican's Managing Director this twa year come Aprile. He did his echteen holes at the gowf club on Monday afternoons, as regular as a wag-at-the-waa. Back at the club-hoose, he took a notion to ring his son at work.

"Son, it's me. I'm up at Glenroyal. Why don't you pick up your mum after work and bring her up here for tea?"

"I was going to take Fiona out tonight for a meal, and then we're going to the rugby club."

"Bring Fiona up here too, sure. They do a very good meal up here you know."

Colin reluctantly agreed. His father had been trying for ages to get him interested in the golf. And to bring Fiona home more. When he got home, Mrs Wetheral was ready to go.

She was very well-dressed, but not over-dressed. Maybe too much make-up, but it all accentuated her very pleasant smile. Too much perfume too, for Colin smelt it before he came in from the hall.

"I've got to get changed first," he said, tossing his car keys down on the hall-stand. "And we won't be picking Fiona up till seven."

"There's a cuppa ready for you in the kitchen," Molly called up the stairs after her son.

It didn't take long to get ready. He lifted a biscuit from the plate left out on the kitchen table, and brought it through to the living room where his mother was sitting. She lit a cigarette, blinked with the smoke in her eyes, and smiled a charming smile at her son.

"What's with all the perfume? Been at the gin again?"

His mother laughed. "G and T doesn't smell, dear; don't you know that? Would you not be better wearing a suit?"

Colin was dressed smartly, but casually, with an open-necked shirt and a sharp crease ironed on his light grey trousers.

"No, dad can bring you back. Fiona and I are going on to the rugby club after."

"How were things at the office today?" she said. Molly always referred to the factory as "The Office" – a good reflection of how little the family business was talked about at home. "Your father will be expecting you both to stay," she continued without waiting for an answer.

The Wetherals' house was a different world from the factory and from the houses in the Claw. Penrith, it was called, after the place Colin's granda came from in the Lake District. Colin never thought much about home or Fiona when he was in work, and he never thought about Ulidican at all when he was at home. Sometimes he would look at Fiona, though, and his mind would wander off to some of the office girls.

Lily had never been up the Cherryhill Road in her life, never mind seen the Wetherals' house. She had a picture of it in her head, however: the size of a city centre department store, with a park of trees and grass round it, and nearly as many folk working about it as there were in the factory. Not even near the truth, that picture. It was big enough, but the only folk that worked there were Mrs Stitt that 'done' for them round the house, and old Jim Byres that kept the garden in order. There was a sweeping avenue up to the front door with a few trees in the front older than the house. Jim used to work in Ulidican himself, but was long past that now. Colin had no memory of any time the garden didn't smell of Jim's pipe.

Lily had a picture of Fiona in her head as well. And it was just as wrong. Although Colin only made mention of her once, when he said she was just a childhood friend, Lily knew rightly she was his girlfriend. And she was fearful of how good-looking she must be. In fact, Fiona wasn't bad looking, but she had a thin face with sharp features like her father, and thin lips too. Not like Lily, with her big brown eyes, compared to Fiona's sharp stony-grey ones.

Colin was starting to make comparisons when he was out with Fiona and their friends. Lily's full cheeks and lips were in a league of their own. "There's some lovely-looking girls work in Colin's place. You'll have to keep an eye on him." Fiona could take such teasing for she didn't think their sort could have any attraction – no class, you see. "They're all right till they open their mouth," Colin would reply.

"Is Barbara not coming then?" His sister was out in the back garden, by herself, playing clumsily with a tennis racket and ball. "She's still got her school uniform on."

"No, could you drop her at Jane's? They're going to do some studying together."

Apart from the odd furtive thought about Lily's best features, compared to Fiona's, Colin wasn't obsessive, not at home anyhow. He would notice the way Fiona's skin hadn't the same rounded lubricated sheen, more sharp and powdery. Sometimes he would get wee flashes of things Lily said, and started wondering how different she was from the rest of her sort. How come somebody could be so good-looking and be a good laugh as well?

"Are you sure he's all right, driving, with his leg only out of plaster a couple of weeks?" Fiona turned round from the front seat and asked Colin's mum. She was in the back, sitting forwards, smiling at the two of them.

"Oh Fiona, love, you just try talking to him. Maybe he'll listen to you."

Colin just smiled, drove a bit faster and winked at Fiona.

She smiled back with tight, pursed lips and gave him a slap on the shoulder.

"Why didn't you put a tie on? They'll not let you eat in the clubhouse without it. Sure I've told you before." Old Mr Colin wasn't as cross as he sounded. He gave off to his son as he kissed his wife on the cheek and squeezed Fiona's arm at the same time. They went on in and sat at a table already set out. The club steward came over with the menus on wee typed sheets and whispered something in Mr Wetheral's ear.

"I told you it was the club rule. Here, if you look in my glove compartment you'll get a spare tie."

Colin wasn't fussed, but took his father's car keys and slipped outside. He came back in later with a dirty great black tie lapped round his neck. The tie seemed to have no connection at all to the sports shirt underneath. Mr Wetheral was more irritated by the way his son was wearing his tie, than he had been when he had none on.

"Colin, is that the only tie you keep as a spare?" Molly asked.

"It's not for this I keep it – it's for funerals." He looked at Fiona and smiled. "When you get to my age, its best to keep a black tie handy."

Michael and Trish were waiting at the crowded rugby club bar for Colin and Fiona. They waved from the far end to catch their eye as they came in.

"Sorry we're late. Parental duties."

"Colin, that's not fair. That was nice of your mum and dad to treat us to tea." Fiona sat down beside Trish and caught her by the elbow as she whispered something in her ear, giggling with her shoulders lifted when she sat back, and nodding at a surprised looking Trish.

"You ready for another, Michael?" Colin took his empty glass and the two of them walked up to the bar where half the team were in a social scrum. Lily, at that moment, lived in a different country and was never further from Colin's thoughts.

Michael Kavanagh was a law student at College in Bigganreek, although he called himself a solicitor when out with company. He was trying to find himself a flat nearer the rugby club – which would be near enough the college too, come to think of it. Now he was in digs off the Mossvale Road. Not the best address in town for a solicitor. Well, it wasn't really digs, it was a friend of his father's – Uncle Peter's – but he just called it his lodgings.

"If I ran into the back of another car because my foot wasn't strong enough yet, would I get the blame?"

"You looking free legal advice again Colin?" Michael said loudly. "If you ran into somebody else from the back, even if you had perfect legs like a hooker's, you'd still be in the wrong." The lads guffawed and broke into a burst of the All-Blacks' Maori war dance, turning with their tongues hanging out towards the row of girlfriends sitting along the back wall. The Claw was further afield than New Zealand to the lot of them.

Back at work themorn's morn, Colin did his rounds in record time. Nae mair nor twathree words wae onie o the section leaders. Till he came to Quality Control, that was. Jack M'Clure went straucht ower to him.

"Any chance o' a move back to ma oul job?"

"What's wrong, Jack? I thought you were getting on all right. You don't want to go back onto the weekly paid staff, do you?"

"It's borin', Mr Colin." Jack rarely gien him his name these days. "They say A'm skivin'. Wait till ye see."

He took an unopened can and whisked through his procedure in three minutes flat. "An' A just need to do one o' these every hour. An' another thing. The boys in the packin' shop say A'm just fillin' in any oul figures at all. A wud far rather be back where there's a bit o' crack – an' plenty o' real work to do."

In the normal run o things, Mr Colin would hae been quite pleased wae such a guid display o the Protestant work ethic. He was getting gye and brooned aff wae Jack but. All he had done for him, and nae thanks. Waur, Jack was very aggressive wae him – the way he talked, and aye eeballing him.

He ettled on talking to Lily aboot Jack's request. Instead o spending a few minutes in her office chatting and looking some figures up (or chatting Lily up and looking at her figure as the girls thocht), he asked Lily to come and see him in his office. Like the offices o all the Wetherals, it was on the top floor. At Ulidican you literally did work your way up frae the bottom. Jack had climbed a few floors, but everybody knew the very top was reserved for the owners.

She was shaking like a leaf whenever she came up. But Colin wasnae sat behind his desk. He came forward smiling and friendly and apened the door for her. "Sit yourself down there Lily." He pointed to a chair in front of his desk, closed the door behind her, and sat on the front corner of the desk, looking down at her flushed, sweaty face.

"What's wrong, Mr Colin?" Her big pleading een gien him an unexpected lift o the hairt.

"Nothing at all, Lily. I just wanted to have a wee word with you about Jack."

Her jaw dropped and she couldnae think what to say.

"He wants to move back to his old job. I just wondered if you had any ideas why he seems not to want to get on in here. He could make a good career out of it - the both of you in fact."

"But Jack's just an ordinary working man, so he is. A mean,

he has his own interests, like."

"He's not annoyed with me or anything then?"

Lily blushed. They had crossed words about Mr Colin's obvious flirting with her. "The talk of the place," he had said.

"No," quo she.

"What about yourself then? Do you like working in the office O.K.?" Colin relaxed inside to match his deliberately relaxed posture.

He wanted to sit and chat to Lily all morning. There was nae doubt he fancied her. If they had a few dates to get it oot o his system, sure there would be nothing wrang in that. He thocht on Fiona. It wasnae as if they were married or even engaged. It would be better for her too, if he got rid of this exotic fascination for Lily by discovering what her faults were. She was bound to hae some, apart frae her background. Not yinst did he think what he was doing was an abuse o power. Mind, neither did Lily.

"Oh I love it here, Mr Colin."

Lily did feel powerfu guilty but. She had never been so close to such a boy before. His lang fine hair on top, wae a shade parting it that needed nae oil to keep it in place. She could see through his thin shirt that he wasnae wearing a vest nor nothing. She wanted to hold him, wae her hand on his shirt, feeling the side o his rib cage. She wanted to feel that soft fine hair - but it wasnae richt.

"Jack'll come round, A'm sure. Mebbe he's just taken a scunner at some o' the other men." Lily stood up and made to go, much to Mr Colin's frustration. "A'll have a wee word wi' him tonight."

"Good. Thanks Lily. And let me know if there's anything I can do – for you as well, you know."

Jack was raging when he fun' out Lily already knew he wanted to quit his job. He bad-moothed the Wetherals, and cursed Mr Colin up and doon.

"There's no need to take it out on me," says Lily. "I don't know what's atein' ye. Ye've a good job and the Wetherals are always good to their workers. Sure haven't ye got offered a house, and the both o' us has got promoted." It was nae guid. Jack had been reared as an only child. Maybe that's what made him be so thran when it came to belonging or joining. A church meeting, a club, the Fleshers & Fowlers Guild – ocht ava. Whatever it was, he felt he was betraying his independence, running wae the herd, taking oaths and that. "Freedom o' Concience," quo he. It was near a religion wae him to hae nane.

"Huh," Jack snorted. "See them stuck-up, hoorin' Wetherals. They'll give ye nathin' for nathin'. It's yer soul they want. An' him! – it's just gettin' his hole he's after."

That was the argument over – and just aboot the courtship too.

Lily stormed off, the tears tripping her. Why was it Jack aye thocht the worst o folk? He taen everything the Wetherals did for some bad purpose. When she defended them she got called for everything.

"And what about oul Mrs Allen, then?" Jack had nae immediate answer for that. Old Mrs Allen round the next street was 92, and the Wetherals lifted and laid her in a taxi to work every day. She sat on her own and folded cardboard boxes – the maist o which had to be re-done anyhow. But she was lonesome and didnae want to quit her job.

"She can have her day here, as long as she wants," Mr Colin explained to Jack when he was working in the packing shop himsel. Later on, when Jack was given the quality control job and was making suggestions about saving waste, Mr Colin elaborated. "Well, it's good for morale. We're proud of the way we look after our most loyal workers."

Jack thocht that keeping him on till he was in his 90s wouldnae be much o a reward.

Despite the row, Lily broke it off wae Jack in her ain time. Pleasantly, wae nae cross words. She took the decision earlier but, and just waited for Jack to put into words what anybody could see was needed. It was the man's place to actually break it off, even when he didnae want to.

Maybe they would get back thegither. Rabbie had asked her out, and if he asked again, she micht just go oot wae him. She was free noo, and could even day-dream about going out wae Colin. Jack was richt in thon regard, for money didnae make you a better person. And she was every bit as good as any of the Wetherals, apart frae fancy claes and guid manners and that. Even if he asked she wouldnae go oot wae him, but it was nice to think he fancied her. And Jack was wrang aboot that. All men were after the yin thing, but Mr Colin liked her for herself. Aa the same, it wouldnae work. Where would they go? Oot wae his friends or back to his hoose to meet the parents? "A hardly think so," she thocht, and Mr Colin didnae seem that much o a hunk in that licht. Maybe Jack wasnae that bad after all. Lily wondered if she had done the richt thing, getting Jack to bust up.

She did it. She never thocht she would hae, and it was like a cure. Colin Wetheral asked her oot and she said no. He never wasted onie time, yinst he learnt that Jack was history. It was done on impulse, but a michty strang yin at that.

"Sure you wouldn't want to be seen at the pictures wi' me," Lily said. "I'm only an ordinary workin' girl ye know."

Colin Wetheral was flattered at the rejection. He taen it as a sort o a compliment. She obviously thocht he was too good for her, and was afeard to get hersel involved. How wrang could he get, but it came natural to him to think that. All his friends thocht, at the back o their heids, they were better than the lower orders. But it was bad form to say it, and even wrang to bring such thochts to the fore. But Lily's coy refusal fired up Colin's imagination to a fu bleeze. Afore the month was oot it had become an obsession, the mair he wasnae going to ask twice.

Lily, and Jack, and all the folk they kent, knowed they were as good as any o the rich folk. At heart they often thocht because they wurnae rich they were better. Sure that's what the Bible says, so it does. And their fancy church-going didnae make a big difference for them did it? Not while they run the big fancy churches anyhow.

"Pip–pip, peep."

Lily and her friends were walking back to the bus-stop after quitting-time, whenever Mr Colin's car sped by. He waved out at the line o them stretched oot the width o the fitpad, and they all waved back, except for Lily. The others grabbed her hand by the wrist and waved it furiously for her at the back o the car. Colin could see this and smiled elatedly as he saw Lily lauching and affrontit at the same time. There was nae taxi for Mrs Allen that day, nor for the next while. Mr Colin would do the evening run, even if it was oot o his way and into strange, mysterious territory.

Mrs Allen had been a widow this fifty year. Her man worked in Ulidican even before auld Mr Colin's day. Some clown had been fooling aroon wae the gate switches on the new factory lift. Twa floor he fell doon the shaft, but eneuch tae kill him. The Allens had leeved in yin o Ulidican's hooses, but the Guild helped Mrs Allen flit to the Claw. Too monie memories o the accident, they said. She wantit to stay working there but, and refused all offers o a new job.

Colin's car was a flashy white Hillman Minx. The sort wae a lang leather front seat – like a bus's only mair springy. And the gear change was a lever on the steering column. There was plenty o cars seen round Fiji Street where Mrs Allen lived, but a big flashy yin aye drew some notice.

"Number 40, son. The same age as maself." She wasnae big at conversation wae Colin, for she was rannering at times. Nae doubt she thocht she was in a taxi.

The minute the car stopped, the dark broon door o No. 40 opened, and a girl came oot to help her in. "Hi, grannie. You're getting some treatment theday, so ye are."

Colin got out too and, wae the help o the girl, oxter-cogged her in through the front door.

"Take her straight through to the back room. M'da has a wee bed set up for the downstairs, an' she's her own wee chair beside it."

"All right Mrs Allen. See you next Tuesday?"

She only worked twa afternoons a week now.

"The box is behind the front door," quo she.

"She thinks you're here to read the meter," the girl said, nodding Colin back through the front kitchen-parlour. "A'm her grandaughter – we just live four doors up. Are you Mr Wetheral?"

"Yes," quo he, returning her relaxed pleasant smile. She was just as guid-looking as Lily, and reminded him of somebody.

"Colin?" she speired again. He nodded, a bit surprised by the familiarity. But then she didnae work for Ulidican, so why should she no be. "The' call me Mavis."

Mavis sat down in the parlour, lounged back in the seat and measured him up wae a smile and her tongue poking a bump in her cheek at the same time. Suddenly she sat up and felt in her pocket. "Cigarette?" she said, pulling twa oot o the packet and reaching one full stretch.

"No thanks, I'm stopped," Colin said, half tempted to start again. But he wasnae sure what he micht be letting himsel in for. Mavis lit up and pointed wae her cigarette for Colin to sit down. He wasnae comfortable in these wee hooses. They were that small, and where did they keep all their claes and stuff? "I'd better get on. Thanks anyway. We think very highly of Mrs Allen you know. So anything else I can do let me know."

Mavis smiled and nodded.

"Thanks again," quo he, fascinated by his ain reaction, in that he didnae think her rude for no thanking him. "I suppose you know Lily Gamble, then?"

As he was about to leave, his thochts had turned to Lily again. She wouldnae be hame yet, for the bus would take that bit longer. Maybe he would spot her going in her ain hoose. Was it the same as Mrs Allen's inside, twa up, twa doon? How could a family o five grown-ups manage?

Mavis shook her heid.

"The Gambles? They live in Samoa Street, I'm not sure what number."

"Na, never heard o' them. Samoa Street's the next one round. Are they relations then?"

He was surprised she could think that, but pleased too. Oot in the street, his car was the centre o attraction for a wheen o noisy weans.

"This your motor mister?"

"Yes," he said, getting his keys out.

"How much did it cost?"

"Over a pound." He wasnae used wae bantering, strange childer, and the pack sensed it.

"What, a fiver?" yin wee lad shouted, and the others lauched. "You a policeman?"

"No," Colin replied, half heartit, and wae his smile straining.

"A film star?" "A soldier?" "An ice-cream man?" Yin by yin they shouted and lauched at their ain jokes.

"A fenian?" the first cheeky wee skitter shouted to even

mair howls o lauchter. He couldnae'a been mair nor nine or ten. Colin's smile disappeared as he got in the car and startit the engine up.

"Hey bai! You! – sling yer hook an' don't come back here without my permission." The warning came frae the mooth o yin o' the weans pointing doon the street. He was small enough to shout through the car window without bending down and had turned aggressive yinst Colin was safely in his car. Then he turned his back on the motor and kicked it wae his heel.

Mavis had heard the noise and came out and scattered the brats as Colin went to move off. She knocked on his window.

"Down the street, turn right and that takes you into Samoa Street, and right again onto the Road." The motor was pointing doon the street anyhow, so he followed the instruction. But he was thinking mair o his car than Lily just noo.

It was a guid three hunner yards afore he came to the only street off to the richt. Then back up Samoa Street he went. The last thing he wanted to see now was Lily, or anybody he knew. There were other streets off to the left, wae a few weans and women at the corner o this yin, and lads wae their hands in their pockets at the next.

"Preeng!" He thocht that a stane had hit the car.

"Preeng! Preeng!" Another twa. The wee skitters were clodding stanes and had hit the side and back o the car. Aff he went, twice the speed, and never stopped till he came to a quiet bit o the city centre.

Oot he got to hae a look. Three small-bore bullet holes. Noo, thon was a real sickener that stopped Colin Wetheral's flirtation wae the Claw stane deid.

Chapter 6

The Test

Annie Kavanagh walked straucht into the Gambles' parlour wae Ernie dozing at the fire.

"Is Lily in?"

Ernie woke up and apened the yin ee.

"Sorry, did A wake ye Mr Gamble?"

"No, A was just restin' ma eyes." Lily came in from the working kitchen.

"Ach, hiya Annie."

"Ye for out thenight, Lily? My Paul's out again and A thought ye cud come round. If ye're not doing nathin' like. Seein' you an' Jack's had a big bust up."

"Well, A'm not sure," Lily started.

"Ach away round," said Ernie. "Sure you're hardly out o' the house these nights."

"Isn't that awful about yer man Mr Wetheral getting shot at an' all? Who do you think done it Lily? My da says the polis'll never rest till the' get them, for somebody has it in for him, an' he says it was the second time the' tried to get him, an' ye don't get away wi' that when it's one of the big bosses."

"Well, Lily's da's here," said Ernie, "an' he says it was just target practice. The' wudn't'a missed if anybody round here was wantin' to get him."

"Or mebbe just to scare him," Lily said as both turned to look at her.

"What wud anybody want to do that for?"

"I dunno." Lily changed the subject. "A'll come round thenight later on, Annie."

Paul was at the Defenders band hall wae Tommy and Lily's brother Billy. He could play the flute proper and read music too, but that wasnae needit. After a few sessions in Cherryhill Silver when Jack taen him, he never went back. He couldnae be bothered learning the fingering for another instrument, and they took it far too serious.

You never really joined the Claw Defenders, you just went along wae somebody you knew. Naebody asked aboot Paul. He leeved in Samoa Street, he was billies wae Tommy and Billy, and his da-in-law was Cooncillor Graham. And he aye wore a blue, black and red City fitbaa scarf under his coat. Just an inch showing round the back o the collar. No ower the top like a fanatic. Maist o all, you could say what you liked to him, and even banter him about him needing to spend years in the confession box. "I can take any religion," he would say, "as long as A don't have to go to church." "Sounds like a good Prod to me," Tommy announced to the band's unofficial committee o inspection. The only qualification needed to join was to want to join. If ye could play, that was a bonus.

But it would be a mistake to think that Paul had turned, just because he got married in Annie's church. He never was a good Catholic, like his mother was. And he liked Protestant churches and clergy even less. At least the oul priests were ordinary folk, like themsels – no after big wages and trying to leeve like lords. And boys but noo he kent only too well that ye couldnae be married, and put other folk first, baith at the yin time. The priests knowed that, but he had made his bed in the Claw, and he would do his best to enjoy lying in it.

The Kavanaghs back in Cavan were sort o ootsiders onie-how. It was put doon to their granda being in the RIC, and then out fechting for the English in World War I. No that they were ever threatened nor naethin. But if they didnae get treated like good Free-Staters, then they would just keep themsels to theirsels. Neither Paul nor his brothers Michael and Peter even thocht o going to chapel any more, but for different reasons.

Paul had half expected the band hall to be maistly folk he had never met afore, but forbye Billy and Tam, and Andy Murphy, there was Skipper McCarroll and Jim Reid frae the fitbaa crowd. And Len Bones stood by himself at the back, and Jimmy Beattie frae his ain work – another prentice spark, and a wheen o others he knowed the faces o.

"Hammermen." Andy Murphy called the tune. "D'ye know it Paul?"

"Ay, fire ahead."

Paul got into the way of it quick eneuch. The flute was aulder, simpler and wee'r nor the yin he had at hame – back in Cavan that is.

"Keep up wi' the drums, Paul," Andy called. Then, as if thinking aloud. "He can handle it bravely, but." Paul was pleased when Andy addressed that verdict to the whole band.

In between tunes, there was a racket o different yins blowing their lip in, practising wee phrases, and just making a noise. Paul tried out the flute they had given him on the "Ballypeden Heroes" and a few others joined in.

Andy nodded to Tam the bass drummer wha gien twa big slaps to call the band to order.

"Ballypeden Heroes," he cried. "And Paul, just play it straight, no fancy bits, it's for marchin' til – not tap dancin'. Take yer time from the drummer, now!"

Twa five beat rolls, four saft verses and four choruses that would hae deeved you, and the Ballypeden Heroes had rid on to another victory. The dynamics were gien by the drummer, that is, the loud and saft verses. You could only play the tune sweetly with yin side drum tapping. Then you had to blaa the best you could when all hell was let rip.

Wae the last note still echoing round the hall, Paul turned to the back, tapping and shaking the water out o the end o his fife. Len Bones wasnae his lone onie mair. Hambo Jack was stood wae his back to the band, shouting into Len's ear.

"Break, lads," Andy cried. Wee Jock Fulton, a short, wiry wee Scotchman wha had a corner shop at the junction o Daisy Street and Solomon Street, went to hae a smoke ootside, in the doorway of the hall. As he passed Hambo he nodded and Hambo winked back. Paul was watching, and caught both Len and Hambo's attention as he raised his flute in a wave. Without returning any acknowledgement, Hambo turned his back on Paul, rudely, and carried on talking to Len. Then he went outside, took offer o a cigarette frae Jock, and in a few drags he disappeared.

"Hasn't Annie and Paul got their wee house lovely?" Ruth said to Lily when the tea and sandwiches were about to kythe frae the back. Lily nodded as she looked round, as if for the first time. She didnae want to say, but lovely as it was, the hoose was ower stiff and formal. It was too tidy for her liking. It wasnae a hame yet.

"Ye have yer house lovely, Annie," Ruth said as the supper tray arrived. "I don't know what yis're goin' to do when ye start a family."

"Oh me and Paul's too house-proud to have childern. And I don't think we'll be here that long anyhow. But if we get our own wee bungalow, you'll still come and visit, won't you?"

"Where would Paul like to live?" Lily was probing for a

weak spot, for she felt a touch patronised by Annie.

"Oh, he's not fussed, so long as he can get to the match on Saturdays. But I think he would just love one o' them wee chalet bungalows the're buildin'. Ye know, outside the city a'thegither."

"Yis're very happy then," Ruth said. "It's lovely to see. Lily, where cud me an' you get a man like that? But then, A wudn't like to leave ma family an' friends an' all."

"Oh you'll soon find the right man, so ye will. And if he really loves you he'll be happy to do what you want." Annie turned her attention on Lily, wha was fu o thocht, eating away at the sandwiches. "Is it all over wi' you an' Jack, Lily?" She lowered her voice to a whisper.

"D'ye think him that was shot – Colin – still fancies ye? Mebbe he'll ast ye out now ye're not goin' out wi' Jack?"

"He wasn't shot, just his car. And if ye must know, he already has ast me out. But A said no." As soon as she had said it, Lily regretted it.

"Had ye finished wi' Jack already, or was that the reason?" Ruth's question was asked in sympathy mair than nebbieness, but baith her and Annie were agog.

Lily's een filled wae tears, and she said naethin. Annie jumped to the wrang conclusion.

"What d'ye mean, the reason? The reason Colin was shot? No! Jack wouldn't. I don't believe it for a minute."

"Don't be daft," Ruth snapped at Annie. "Sure wasn't Jack on his way home from work when it happened. And anyway, Jack would never get himself mixed up wi' anything like that."

"I'm sorry, Lily – I didn't mean it like that. But d'ye think it would put Colin off askin' ye out agane?"

"A don't care," Lily blurted out as Ruth took her cup out o her hand, "A don't want to go out wi' him."

After a minute's reflection, Ruth speired, "And what about

Jack, wud ye go out wi' him agane?"

"A don't know," she said, then shook her heid. "No, it wudn't be fair."

"Yis're so lucky, so yis are, the both o' ye." Ruth's desperation for romance was matched by a list o self-imposed exclusions. And anybody that asked her oot would hae to pass all those tests afore she would even agree to date. But it didnae matter much, for naebody had showed onie interest anyhow.

Lily and Ruth got up to go when they heard the soond o the front door apening.

"Ye don't have to go when Paul comes in. Stop on a while, sure."

Paul came in with Billy Gamble nervously in tow. "All right if we come in too?"

"Of course, pet, bring Billy in – would yis like a wee drop o' tea?" Annie's face fell after Paul nodded Billy in and said, "Skipper and Tam's comin' too – they're just away for fish suppers. Ye cud'n butter a plate o' bread for us an' all?"

"Ye can't bring the whole flute ban' in here – what d'ye think this is?"

"Ach, away on, sure we're better here than down in the Bull." Annie stomped oot to the new working kitchen, longing mair than ever for the day o their next flitting.

"Where's Ken thenight?" Ruth asked Billy, hoping he might be dropping in too.

"A think he's in the house." He didnae explain mair. Ruth kent fine well Ken wasnae in the band, and Billy kent fine well Ruth had Ken down as a possible.

"Bout ye, Lily," Tam said wae a big grin and a wink. When he was sat down he looked as if he micht still hae the bass drum under his T-shirt. "What about you an' me goin' down the town Saturday night?"

Lily just smiled and gien him a "catch-yerself-on" look.

But that only encouraged him. "There's not enough sates in here – c'mon an' sit on ma knee an' ye can feed me ma chips."

Ruth and Annie were the only twa that didnae lauch. Annie was worried about the hoose, and its plunging standards. Ruth was worried that the company was aboot to start using language and drink. And naebody ever teased or flirted wae her.

When Billy looked ready to go, Lily got up. "Thanks Annie. That was great crack. See ye soon." Ruth had left earlier, shortly after Skipper took off to catch the others at the Bull. Only Tam sat on as if he intended to stop the nicht.

Annie was mortified when the peelers arrived at the door. The yae saving grace was that Ruth and Lily had gone hame.

"William 'Skipper' M'Carroll in here?"

"No, he just left half an hour ago."

"Well, ye'll not mind if we take a wee look then." It wasnae a question, or if it was, it was asked after the two peelers had pushed into the kitchen parlour. They had Dear knows the number o layers o waterproof uniform on as they came fistling in. The first yin was fat and red o face, and taen his hat off wae yin hand as he came through. The other was younger, and kept his hat on.

"You Paul Kavanagh then?"

"Yes, what's wrang?"

"I was toul M'Carroll was here, along wi' you and others out of the band hall."

"What d'ye want wi' Skipper?"

"Never you mind, son. Who's this then?"

"That's just Tom Nelson; he's in the band too."

"And what do you play, Nelson?"

"He plays the big drum."

"Can he not answer for himself?" Without waiting for an answer, he speired at Paul. "And what about M'Clean, Jack M'Clean?"

"He's not here, sure he's not in the band – not ours anyhow."

"So ye know him then?" Again, without waiting for an answer he put his cap back on his heid and turned to go.

"Would you not like a wee cup of tea, officer?" Annie asked, still wringing her hands non-stop.

"No thanks, love, maybe next time."

And they were off into the black, where they had come frae.

The polis never used to be that rude, so Annie thocht. She was shocked wae the visitation, but little did she know she had much, much waur to come.

"I'm going to speak to my father about them ignorant lumps," quo she.

"Don't you bother yer arse," said Paul. "What's your da gonna do?"

When Annie thocht about it, her father micht just make things worse, and her mother would die off if she knew. Paul didnae like it ava. It seemed like the peelers were mair suspicious o him leeving in the Claw than onie o his neighbours.

But the polis wurnae the only thing that was changing in the Claw. The firms that had the tens o thousands o hooses bigged in the first place were all run doon. Them as had guid jobs worked across the city, or even oot o it a'thegither. And they had motor cars noo, but nae place to put them at nicht, bar the street. It wasnae safe for the weans to play in the street any more. What wae cars non-stop up and doon, and shoppers on the Road parked baith sides, you would hardly'a knowed the place.

But the biggest change was folk leaving the Claw. Not just to flit to other streets, but to new jobs and hooses miles off in places like Newbiggins, or auld touns like Ballypeden. At the foot o the Claw – the end innermaist the city centre – the redevelopment had started. There was hooses wae wee gardens an big wide streets, and loads o dead-ends like Orchard Close, for the pensioners.

Then the next twathree streets would hae their doors and windows bricked up and the slates off, waiting on their turn. The folk oot o these hooses were all shiftit – just tempo-rary-like – to new cooncil housing schemes at the ootmaist end o the city. Maist would never come back, and the plan-ners couldnae hae squared it anyhow if they had wanted to. But some o the auld folk micht, and their childer wae their childer's childer would stop on in the new schemes and visit the new parts o the Claw in their new cars, and take their parents shopping at weekends awa frae the Road.

Wha wantit to "Save the Claw" anyway? It was a lost cause afore it startit. Any fool can see it noo, but in them days nae-body did. The schools, churches, guilds, halls o ilka kind, and the hooses – all bigged for folk wae nae motors and nae need o them. Just yin reason for the hale clamjamphrey, and that was to hae workers at hand for the big mills and factories. When the jobs went, nae amount o planners, cooncils, guid works o the heidyins o the chapters and guilds, social workers, church inquiries or even a backlash frae the residents and tenants associations, guilds and whatever, could turn the tide.

Sae, whenever the police came to Annie's door, there was a new sense o jitters aboot the place. The auld loud-moothed confidence was still there, but you kent fine the Claw's days were numbered. Naebody knew for why, but, and them that had to would fecht and defend it to the last bullet and the last bottle o stout. Wae sae much suspicion roon aboot, the auld enemy was thocht the waur o. If there was an attack frae the Mossvale Road, they would get what they got be-fore. Everybody had mind o the trams, and what way you had to lie doon on the decks when there was snipers firing. The auld folk aye said the snipers fired frae the roofs o the chapels, but there was hardly onie on a guid line o sicht frae the Mossvale Road.

Noo that there was nae war on and nae industry, the authorities had little need o the Claw, and suspicion was riz on baith sides. If the troubles were going to start up again, the womenfolk maun stock up wae breid, and the men wae guns. Rumours o this and whids o that. Paul would likely not be trusted till he was tested.

Annie saw a hearse wae a coffin in the back stop on the Blackfort Road. The driver asked for directions to the Mossvale Road. He got shown the way wae respect, but only after the driver was made to get out and apen the coffin to reveal the corpse. Then an apology and explanation – "ye never know these days – guns, like." Annie was affrontit but it was a sign o the times.

Such uncertainty came in ups and doons. The auld symbols were still there, comforting gable paintings done by the boys o the Loyal and Ancient Guilds. These were timeless splashes o bricht heirskip. At the junction of Captain Street and Samoa Street was a painting o the Claw Defenders platoon up an oot o the trenches at the Somme. Doon baith sides was a scroll o names of them that died frae Samoa Street and Solomon Street alane. Twenty seven names, counting Pte. Stanley Bates. Doon Captain Street was a pair o gavels either side o the road, between each side street cutting across. Not all o them had paintings, but that was the best road if you wanted to see a selection. Like the 'Biggin o the City Walls' (it didnae say if it was Jericho or Jerusalem or Derry), or Oliver Cromwell wae fiercesome warts, swords and all, or wee Jenny clodding her three-legged creepie stool at some oul bishop. Wae history like that behind you, could you ever imagine a day when the Claw would be gutted?

The polis didnae come back to Samoa Street till after the

guilds' fair day. If the Claw's sense o security came in ups and doons, the fair day was the big up o the year.

Frae the scraich o day auld men in full regalia met up wae others wae their regalia still lapped up in broon paper bags. Weans raised black stour frae the ashes o the street bone-fires and got shouted at. The Guild o Fleshers and Fowlers, Jack's Guild, was gathering at the other end o town, in the Brickworks area. Here was the Shipwrights and Steelmen – the S.S. men as Ernie called them – "Loads o' Saturdays and Sundays overtime." Mind, he used to be in that yin himsel. And there was Samuel Agnew, like a city gent wae white gloves and rolled up umbrella, looking for the rest o the Total Abstinence Independent Guild. Everywhere men met up with brother guildsmen they hadnae seen frae last year. If the modern technological revolution was bleeding the Claw to death, its life-blood was pouring back in for the day. Years back, the folks gathering had only to step oot the door. Now, mair and mair were coming back to a reunion and to pay homage to their tribal homeland. Bandsmen wae bricht red, and black, and blue uniforms were gathered in clumps, and by half-echt, guild banners were taen frae agin hooses, un-furled, and bands wae guild chapters behind snaked in and oot, till they all came thegither at the Blackfort Road Guild Hall, for the big parade. Thoosands and thoosands o folk, here, there and everywhere. Mair excitement than ocht you could imagine. It was Paul's first, actually walking that is. Onie guild he could hae joined wouldnae be oot on this day and they had different pictures o history. But the bands could hae oniebody in them ava.

Flute bands o young bucks, siller bands o men wae glasses footerin wae music cards, kilty pipe bands, accordion bands o wee girls in tartan mini-skirts, and wee lads running roon lost wae band caps and jackets far too big for them. And bricht siller and brass instruments, buckles, swords, pikes, and badges all glinting and gleaming.

And it was the first time frae they were married that Paul cleaned his ain shune. Then Annie gien them a dicht as well.

Excitement ower, dust and stour settled, and his sair feet soaked in a bath, Paul was wrecked. It was a lang walk to the Fair Hill Field and back. Ay, being part o it made ye feel brave and good, but you only seen your ain wee bit, before ye and just behind. Not like other years when he could stand and watch the hale lot frae the fitpad.

Later on in the month, the terminal illness the Claw was suffering from got a firmer grip. The flags, bunting and triumphal arches that decorated every street for the entire month o the July Fair were still up, but then back to porridge it was. Wae the holiday fever past and gone, the bunting started to look tired. The cancer o development spread decay in front o it, and mair suspicion. And another visit to Paul and Annie's frae the polis.

If the first visitation wae the peelers was half-polite, the second was scary-rude. Only twa bust into the hoose, another twa were stood ootside wae rifles.

"Where is it then, Kavanagh?"

"Where's what?"

But they had started pulling open doors, lids, curtains, pushing chairs around, and pushed Annie too when she scraiched, "What is it? What is it? Yis can't just come in my house like that." She screamed again, quiet-like, for it was done wae the breath taen in.

"D'ye know who my father is? Councillor Graham. Ye can't just come bustin' in here wi'out a warrant."

"I don't care who yer da is." The peeler looked gye and angry at even being talked to. He turned his back on Annie as he spake, and telt the other yin to make a search o the back yard.

"Check under every bit o' dirt."

It was Paul, no Annie, that lost the heid at that point.

"Houl on now, yis are way out o' order. I know the law – where's yer search warrant?"

"Just you sit down there Kavanagh and shut yer face. Ye're not in the Free State now. The only people wants search warrants is them wae something to hide."

The other policeman called frae the yard, "Out here, Jim," and for a few minutes Annie and Paul were alone. They just looked at each other but, and Paul shrugged his shoodhers at his wife's questioning glare.

"OK, when did ye get the coal delivered?"

Annie answered, the mair the question was speired at Paul, wae the aggressive peeler's face stuck twa inches in front o his nose.

"Months ago," quo she, "we haven't hardly had the fire lit this summer – just the electric one."

The other policeman spoke for the first time.

"Could anybody come in your yard without you knowing?"

"A suppose the' could," Paul said.

"But not shovel loads o' coal?"

"Nobody's been at our coal," Annie said. "I would know straight off."

"So how did these get there then, right at the bottom?" He threw two small cloth bags on the table, covered wae coal dust, and shook the contents onto Annie's clean table cloth. Yin bag had teens o wee bullets that rolled this way and that. The tither had a revolver. Annie gasped again and started to shake and greet.

"A never seen them before," Paul said. "The' must'a been in wi' the coal when it come."

"Ay. An' the coal come two months ago. An' this gun

was used a couple o' weeks back. How d'ye explain that Kavanagh?" As he spoke, he smelt the barrel, looked inside, and clicked the trigger to make sure it wasn't loaded. "Is that your initials on the barrel?"

"Where?" Paul said, taking the gun by the handle when it was offered to him. He held it close to his een, and rubbed the side of the barrel wae his left hand. "That's not even letters, it's numbers."

The peeler took the pistol back carefully by the tip of the barrel and put it back in the bag wae a sleekit, satisfied smirk.

"A think you'd better come down the barracks wi' us, till we get a few answers."

As they marched Paul down the street, nebby neighbours disappeared behind closing doors. Annie was scraiching and sobbing at the yin time. "He's not going without me."

"You just go back inside, Mrs, and close your door."

Iris Gamble came out and put her heavy, comforting arms round Annie to restrain her.

"It's all right, love, just c'mon inside our house a minute, and we'll get it sorted out."

Paul was no dozer. He kent he was being set up, but wha would do it? They kept him in a back lock-up in the barracks for hours. Then he was brocht oot again for questioning.

"Whereabouts were you on the last Thursday in June, just after half four?"

Paul needed to think, or rather to get a handle on what was going on, afore he got in onie deeper. "Look, A know nathin' about thon oul gun. A don't want to answer any questions till A've talked to my brother."

"Ye'll not do yerself any good wi' that attitude. Ye're not talking to nobody but me for the time being. Now, were ye at work that day?"

Paul shrugged his shoodhers and gien grudging, yin-word

answers to everything asked o him.

"When can A talk to my brother?"

"When ye get out, in about 12 years."

"But he's a lawyer. A thought I was allowed a phone call."

"What's his name? You've been watching too many pictures. I'll check out who ye can speak to when we charge ye."

"Charge me? What with?"

"We're spoilt for choice," the policeman said.

"Take him back; maybe a few days on his own will loosen his tongue."

In about three hours, just before midnight, the painted iron door of the lock up opened again. Paul's brother Michael came in, and the door was left open behind him.

"You all right, Paul?"

"Ay, but – what's going on?"

"It's O.K. Ye'll be getting out wi' me just now, for a day or two anyhow."

"What d'ye mean a day or two? Can you do solicitor for me?"

"I'll sort ye out wi' somebody, don't worry."

It would do later for Michael to explain why he couldn't act as Paul's solicitor. He had already been asked by Colin Wetheral, as a favour, to advise him about keeping the police on the hunt for whoever was trying to shoot him. The minute he had heard Paul was lifted, Michael told Colin to get his own family solicitor on the job. But he still might have a conflict of interest if he was to officially represent his brother. Truth was, he wasn't a fully fledged solicitor yet.

Back at home for a precious few days, Paul was told that, guilty or innocent, he would be in jail on remand for a year at least. And that was afore he would get the chance o a trial. The yin man he had to see quick was Len Bones. He would hae all the answers.

Richt eneuch, Len Bones did.

"Ye'll be all right. Take it easy. Just say nathin'. No matter what the' ast ye. If ye do exactly what I say. A promise ye. Ye'll be all right – an' yer house, an' Annie. An' ye'll be back home a free man in a matter o' weeks."

Len seemed really friendly for the first time. But Paul would hae been an eejit to trust him, and that he wasnae.

"How come the gun was in the coal you delivered then?"

"A swear it wasn't there when A brung the coal. It's the peelers, the' must have plantit it to set ye up."

That seemed plausible eneuch, for the polis were fit for it. But how come they kent where to come til?

"I know ye're not mixed up wi' anything," Len said. "Ye will be all right but. Just say nathin'. Whatever the' ast ye, just say 'Nothing to say' – nathin' else, not even the time o' day, or the'll twist it an' stitch ye up in court."

"But what about Annie? She's near in hysterics."

"A give ye ma word, Annie'll be all right. Where was she whenever ye come back from the barracks? Wasn't she bein' looked after?"

True enough, when Paul came back hame, his ain hoose was empty. He thocht she maun hae went hame to her ma's, but he fun' her at Lily's. There she was wae her face swole wae greeting, and a hoosefu o neighbour womenfolk keeping her company. They really did feel sorry for her. Onie o them would hae been affrontit wae such a scandal – but Annie!

"An' here's Paul now, love – A toul ye it would be all right."

But Annie just girned all the more, and hardly had the strength to hold onto Paul's neck. He was a wee bit gunked that they only seemed glad to see him back for Annie's sake.

"It's O.K., I'm all right too," quo he sarcastically.

The womenfolk wanted to hear all the details. Ernie listened quiet in the background. He alone kent how Len Bones had put the gun under the coal – and it wasnae because he had anything to do wae it himsel.

Len's brother, Mal, had a magic trick he did, whiles, in the barber's shop. You had to pick oot a coloured marlie frae a box – all different – and Mal would make it disappear. Then he brung out a ball o wool, unwound it, and at the middle was a match box, wae your marlie inside. Ernie kent hoo he done it. He had a wee pipe into the half apen box, and then wool wound round the lot, wae the end o the pipe sticking oot. So in he rolled the marlie, and oot he would pull the pipe, through the wool that just closed ower. He knowed there was some reason for Len Bones leaving thon oul pipe o his sticking up oot o the back corner o Paul and Annie's yard, and just piling the coals up roon it.

But Ernie said nothing. Nothing ava. And Annie could say nothing to her ain folks, for fear o what they micht say. And Paul could say nothing ava to the polis. He had nae choice. It wasnae wha he could maist trust, it was wha he trusted the least.

But what was the reason? To test his loyalty? To gie the Claw a permanent hold on him? Or to redd the Claw o Paul and his likes, and get the Samoa Street hoose freed up again? Only Len Bones and Hambo Jack knowed the answer to that.

Chapter 7

Time and Motion

It's odd the way the upstairs o buses fill up, and where folk sit. First they sit at the windows up the left hand side, mair or less every other seat, and then up the windows on the richt hand side. You just head for the middle o the bit where there's naebody roon ye. Like colonising a beach at holiday time. Jack didnae see oniebody he knew, and at ganging-tae-work time you never really wanted to hear much crack oniehow. Sae he just sat where there was naebody front or back, on the richt hand side o the bus. If Lily got on, she would sit doonstairs. And now they were split up, he didnae want to be sitting looking doon at her if she was at her stop.

That was why it was odd that when Joe Stitt got on, he sat in the empty seat in front o Jack. There was plenty o other seats higher up the usual preference list. He was being friendly. Joe turned round wae his arm along the top o the double seat, and his back to the passing traffic.

"Well Jack, what's the crack?"

"Dead on, Joe." Jack seized the opportunity to ask a favour. "Ye cudn't put in a word for us to get back to the packing floor, could ye?"

But by now the top deck was full, and Joe turned round

when the last seat beside him got taken. When they both got off, clumping doon the stairs, Lily and twathree friends had just got off in front. Joe tugged on Jack's sleeve to stop him, as he gien his saved cigarette butt a licht.

"Wetheral thinks you have it in for him. How come? He sez he had big plans for ye."

"Oh ay, he's got big plans all right. But for himself." Joe just looked at him, and walked on to catch up wae the girls.

"Wud you get aff!" Lily guldered at him when he catched her frae behind and lifted her off her legs. Joe lauched and walked on ahead, firing his butt right across the street wae a flick o his second finger and thumb. Sparks flew when it hit the window o a parked car.

Joe Stitt was aye in good form when he was in control. He was waiting on Colin Wetheral ootbye his office door whenever he swanned in about ten past nine. Mr Colin was pleased to see him too.

"Ah Joe, the very man. Any news on the Jack M'Clean front?"

"A'm sure he knows the buddy that done it all right, but it looks like it wasn't him."

"Well, the fellow the police lifted certainly wasn't the right one. There's something funny going on there."

"A'll tell ye one thing, Mr Colin, ye'd need to keep an eye on M'Clean anyhow."

"He's asked to get back to the shop floor."

"Ay, well, as A say, I'd keep him separate from the rest o' the men. It's up to yerself, but, so it is."

"What about a spell out at Ballypeden?"

Joe screwed his face up as if he'd just ate something nasty. The branch factory in Ballypeden was nae answer.

"Or could I put him along with the Efficiency Consultants?"

It wasnae really management asking Joe Stitt's opinion

on how to run the place. Colin was just thinking aloud. An American firm of Management Consultants, Scrievner-Tibbles Inc., were coming to do a work study on the whole factory.

"It's the sort of thing we could do ourselves, if we had the time. They say they guarantee their fees will be covered by efficiency savings. And we get a grant for most of their costs from the Ministry of Industry." It was an honest report that management gave the workers – or rather Joe Stitt and a few other Guild representatives – but they all looked suspicious.

Mr Colin thocht they jaloused they wurnae being told the whole story, and that's why they seemed unexcited.

"Actually, the fees they charge will be notionally higher – on paper," he had told Joe on the Q.T. It was a vain attempt to put minds at rest by being totally honest, in a perverse sort o a way, "and so the grants will cover the lot."

"Ye mean we'll get less money for the same work?"

"No, you'll get more money for more work – well, not actually more *work* – for more output. I mean, with increased efficiency, the same effort, the same work, will produce more, and then there'll be bigger bonuses."

"We all goin' on piece work then?"

"Well, anybody that wants to earn bonuses."

Joe didnae fancy the idea o American Time and Motion experts coming in. But if the Wetherals had worked out some dodge wae the Ministry of Industry, the thing was unstoppable. The best he could hope for was to get a good handle on it. He had been looking for some way.

"That's the thing, Mr Colin, put M'Clean along wi' the Time and Motion boys. Ye'll soon see then if he's workin' for ye or agin ye."

"I'll have to think about it."

"Don't forget ye have to get this whole Time and Motion

thing passed by the Guild before ye can start."

Mr Colin gien Joe a studied look. For a minute he thocht Joe was getting a wee bit upitty. Joe twigged, and winked to indicate he could fix it.

"Just get me a few details before the next Chapter meetin'."

Mr Colin seemed reassured.

"And A suppose ye would want a Guilder for the liaison officer anyhow, like the last time. An' who better?"

The first Jack learnt o getting shiftit was frae Joe Stitt.

"How come ye weren't at the Chapter last night?"

"A can't get. Sure it's the same night as the ban'."

Jack thocht it was a bit rich, coming frae Joe Stitt that was hardly ever at the Guild o Fleshers and Fowlers. Onie time Jack had been, there wasnae sicht nor soond o him. "The oul F'ers," Joe called them, and he wasnae usually one for abbreviations.

"A think I've ye set up for a move all right, an' a right cushy number too. But ye'll have to wait till A see Wetheral agane."

"Back to the packing?"

"No. Just wait an' see. It could be yer best move yet, but. So just remember who gat ye it."

Mrs M'Clean was that proud o her big son and his new job, in an office, wae Americans. And wae thon wee doll frae the Claw oot o sicht, afore ower lang, maybe she would be history and all. But Jack's mother hadnae the length o her son. Wha could ever forget their first girlfriend – especially yin that gien ye the elbow?

But there Jack was, in the old Quality Control office wae a big table moved in and four seats round it, for there wasnae room for a wheen o desks. The table was square, but whatever end Mr Tibbles sat at was the top. But he never came mair nor yinst or twice. Sandy Robson, the handyman joiner that made bits and pieces for the machines, did repairs etc, couldnae stand the American. Well, Mr Scrievner was nae problem, for he never turned up ava. Mr Tibbles, but, had a beard, dark Mediterranean skin, and bulging broon een like Bluebeard.

"C'mon, Tibbles, pussy, pussy," Sandy would say when his back was turned, making a rubbing gesture with his thumb and first two fingers as if he was footering wae his baird, or calling a cat.

At first Jack liked the new job. Mr Tibbles hardly was there. When he was he hardly spoke. The other two wurnae Americans ava, the mair they baith pit on a bit o a drawl, seeing they'd been there for training. Tim McKearney was a coorse sort frae up country, red-faced and over-weight. He never seemed to stare back at the girls the way Tibbles did, but he aye made coorse remarks aboot them to Jack. McKearney's big problem was his nose. He was aye hoaking at it wae a hanky, and giein it a blow when he could find a dry corner. Whiles his hay fever was that bad he had wet hankies hanging all roon the office to dry.

"It's never hay fever. Ye must be allergic to some o' the food stuff in the factory," he was told. At times the office looked like a Chinese laundry. The only time he cleared the room was when Tibbles turned up.

Not that Sandy was a saint himsel, but he was vicious aboot the way Tibbles would stand in the middle o the processing lines, eyeing up the youngest and best looking girls one at a time, bold as brass. The sicht o Tibbles turned general suspicion into universal dislike. Of the Scrievner-Tibbles trio, only Josh Carruthers was mildly human and likeable. He was English, or had an educated English accent, but told everybody he was American. Jack thocht he was Jewish, for yin time he mentioned the Guild, Josh said "There's a lot more to religion than that you know." Then he put his thumb behind a tie pin he was wearing in the shape of a six pointed star. "Do you know what that is?" Jack didnae like to say "the Star o' David?", so he just shrugged his shoodhers. "We must have a talk about religion some time," Josh said.

Tim McKearney's dislike o the Guilds was ethnic rather than ocht to do wae ethics.

"The Guilds' parade – have ye ever seen it?" Jack said yin day to them all when Tibbles had made some remark about not being told he had bloody secret societies to deal wae. "It's the biggest festival in the British Isles." Tibbles just stared at Jack over his dilated, sneering nostrils.

Tibbles turned away in disinterest. But Tim was even mair red-faced than usual. "You want to travel around the worl' and broaden your mind," he snapped at Jack. "Have ye ever seen the Mardi Gras?" That was the nearest they got to talking politics or religion, apart frae ootside o hours.

The chippie on the Blackfort Road was an occasional stop off for Jack on his way back hame frae the band practice. Yin nicht he went in on the spur of the moment to get a fish supper. At yin o the side tables was Josh Carruthers, casually dressed, drinking a bottle o coke through a straw. He looked oot o place there, on his ain.

"You not speaking, Jack?" he asked. It was an unavoidable invitation to sit doon and join him.

"What are you doin' here?" Jack said. He felt gye uncomfortable in his company oot o working hours, and especially near his hame.

"Just passing through. You're not in a hurry are you?"

"Na, not really."

Jack spent the next half an hour trying to get oot o an intense conversation wae Josh. There's a time and a place for everything. Jack liked Josh. In fact, he was the only yin o the team he thocht wasnae cut-ye-short rude. Natheless, when Josh started talking aboot the richts and wrangs o the

Guild, wae people standing in the queue beside wae their lugs twitching, it was time for off.

Jack couldnae care less about improving efficiency at Ulidican, nor making a career. Nor the Guild for that matter. But he was gye sair for months aboot getting the push frae Lily. That's what was in his mind a guid part o the day. Avoiding her that is, for she had started going oot wae another fella. It got that he was near as feard o going into the dispatch office wae Lily in at her desk as he was o going into the chippie when Josh micht be there.

He was after other girls – he wasnae obsessed wae Lily the way Colin Wetheral was getting – but his mind just kept wandering in her direction. Tim McKearney learnt him how to work this strange clip boord wae a lever that had three stop watches alang the top. Whenever you squeezed a lever at the side o the clip boord, another lever pressed the top o each watch at the yin time – starting yin, stopping the next, and putting the other back to nocht. Jack thocht Lily's da would be interested in how it worked. Dear knows what Ernie could do wae such a clever wee idea. It meant you could time parts o jobs without losing the fraction o a second between stopping, returning and starting again on the yin watch. Mr Colin didnae like the clip boord. Certainly, it was in the girls' faces when a wee watch wasnae. But Jack didnae like Mr Colin, and it made him look professional, the mair he was just a trainee.

Twa months at this and Jack had had eneuch. He was at the ruch edge, doing management's dirty work, and had to take abuse frae the girls when they heard all the time they were getting allowed to handle each can, or box, or label. Sandy had to make these wooden extensions, specially designed by Josh, roon each work station. These shelves could hold bits and pieces nearer to the line, and cut doon the length o movements each wee action taen. And all to cut a few seconds aff the measured time for the job. Every day he spent langer and langer in Sandy's workshop or walking round the factory, quickly, wae his clip boord under his arm, to avoid the hard-case time and motion jobs.

Joe Stitt lost interest in the whole operation. His job was a bit o this and a bit o that, moving things maistly. It wouldnae be timed oniehow. So he just carried on as if the Americans were in the way. The sooner they were gone the better. Tibbles was a different sort o scary-rude to what Joe Stitt was. The only time they crossed swords was when Tibbles was doing his high Admiral bit – stood in the main passageway through the canning line, staring roon the floor at the girls. Joe came up behind him wae a pallet truck and near took the heels aff him. Tibbles made eye contact wae Joe for this first time, expecting an apology.

All he got was a mouthful o abuse for getting in the road. The earlier burst o friendliness wae Jack had gone too. He treated Jack and what he was doing as if he was letting the side down. And Jack felt he was too.

There was strains wae the Wetherals and the Work Study exercise forbye. They couldnae mind a time when there was such a bad atmosphere wae the workers. Mr Colin got embarrassed when he fun' himsel haeing to explain 92-year auld Mrs Allen to Tibbles, and fun' himself acting as a go-between for the Guild wae him – instead o the other way roon.

"It's a family firm," auld Mr Colin said to his son. "Ye won't get the best out o' the workers by timing every turn of the hand. No more than you would in a family."

Colin Wetheral wished the whole exercise was over too. He was being treated like a child in his own firm by people getting paid to modernise. He even fun' himsel trying to look busy and no spend ower lang in the dispatch office talking to

Lily. And Jack M'Clean was getting mair and mair shirtier, he thocht. He just didnae trust him, and told Joe Stitt so.

"Well, put him back at the packing then," Joe said.

"But what about the Work Study Team?"

"Send them packin' an' all."

Mr Colin smiled and walked back to the dispatch office.

Paul was back in on remand when the second shooting happened. Richt ootside the Ulidican director's entrance this was – the yin only used by Tibbles and the Wetherals. Yin bullet through the windscreen o Tibbles's hired car, shattering it.

"Pity it was empty," Joe Stitt said to Mr Colin, who was genuinely horrified. "Only jokin', now," he added when he saw the reaction.

"That's nothing to joke about Joe. Right in broad daylight. How do you know it wasn't meant for me again?"

"Well, the one thing ye know is that Jack M'Clean was here in work whenever it happened – like the rest o' us."

"I hope the men don't see me as trying to break the Guild. I don't have any problem with it you know."

Jack kent he couldnae ask for a shift again, but even quality control was better than the work study. And Mr Colin wasn't exactly friendly this weather. The rest o the employees were in a stramash aboot the shooting – they all thocht it was a desperate thing, and even Joe Stitt never tried to justify it. But the atmosphere oot on the floor was bad, and waur getting.

"Come."

Jack thocht he heard Mr Colin answer when he knocked on his office door, but he wasnae sure. He gien it another knock.

"Come." It was louder and impatient this time. When Mr Colin saw it was Jack, he got a bit jumpy and rose frae his seat.

"Well? What is it?"

"A've come to give in ma notice." Jack could hardly believe

he had done it. He thocht it would hae been harder than being interviewed for the job in the first place.

Mr Colin's face changed expression over and over, like pictures on a rolling drum, as the thochts tumbled in his mind. Then he catched himsel on and smiled, warmly, sympathetic-like.

"We'll be very sorry to lose you, Jack. Have you got another job somewhere else?"

Jack hadnae thocht that yin out. He had twathree notions, but this was on the spur o the minute, and he was mair ready for telling Wetheral where he could stick his tin cans.

"A'm thinkin o' joinin' the police."

That surprised the baith o them. Mr Colin aye thocht Jack would end up at the wrang end o the Laa – no in the polis. And Jack just said the first thing that came into his mind, by way o a smairt answer that would get up Wetheral's neb.

In the cold licht o day, but, Jack walked oot o Ulidican for the last time wae nae job and nae prospects. And a hairt that was jumping wae joy. Free at last, free at last.

Jack was a wakerife sort o a body getting, these twathree years frae he was left school. But this nicht he slept weel, like the sleep o the deid.

Chapter 8

Newbiggins

It was a cold, sterile, hoor's ghost of a place, with hundreds of avenues, snaking like rivers of concrete this way and that. The estate was soulless, everything a cheap imitation of nature. The main roads of the new housing scheme seemed to wind unnecessarily. Even where there were grass edgings and spindly tree stumps, it was still nothing like the real countryside. Behind concrete flags, footpaths – and gardens big enough for a wee lawn or a tree of your own if you wanted it – were the whitewashed, pebble-dashed houses. Set right back, the council houses curved into wee side avenues, with more off them again – Crescents and Gardens – like branches forking off a big tree. And a great big open grass area in the middle with old trees dotted here and there. The lines of concrete flags that struck straight-line paths across the Green were not out of place. It was about as natural-looking as a golf course. Newbiggins seemed like a grand recreation park. Or a redundancy package that city planners hoped would make this army of Claw folk eternally grateful.

It was winter time when the M'Cleans flitted from the Claw to 39 Rosedown Gardens (*Rizdoon Gairdens*, the unofficial bilingual signs had mistakenly translated it as). The grass cover on the open Green and along the verges of the footpaths was long past its last cut. Not to be walked on if you didn't want to test your shoes for leaks, or go on your ear. To Jack this was what living in the country must be like. Everything was that blasted open. Outside the house there was no sense of being closed in by walls and streets. No, it was nothing like the real country, those fields and dykes and lanes and stone farms that had been bulldozed to make way for the designer housing scheme of Newbiggins.

The M'Cleans were no different from the rest of the Blackfort Road folk that had been re-housed in Newbiggins. Nobody wanted to admit it wasn't all an improvement on the old. The houses were new, or near new, by the time the M'Cleans flitted, but the rents were dearer. And their old bits of furniture and ornaments were out of place.

"H.P. doesn't staun for Half Price, ye know," Jack's dad said every time a new purchase was planned. And the wind and rain. There was no shelter, with gales whipping along the avenues and across the open spaces.

"Ach you're an oul misery guts, John, sittin' there wi' yer cap on every time money's mentioned." Bessie M'Clean half-knew there was some connection between the duncher and the new insecurity. The houses were far apart and cold – concrete everywhere. No longer the cozy, crowded streets of warm-red bricks. The people were far apart too. Maybe Christmas would help them feel at home again. Or maybe they would get to hate the glass-fronted fire even more.

When Jack came down the stairs, his father was raking out the ashes from the smokeless, shut-away fire. He was on his knees, with the glass door open and a newspaper laid out on the hearth for the ashes.

"Where's Ma?"

"She's feelin' bad, so A just toul' her to stay in bed. A've made yer piece. It's on the side in the kitchen." John M'Clean might have retired, but he was full of energy still. The new house was the object of most of his attention, but it was unknown for him to do anything in the kitchen.

"Ma'll kill ye if ye burn the good carpet," said Jack. "Them papers'll burn th'ough."

"Where's the bucket then? A left it out in the back garden beside the coal bunker an' somebody's knocked it aff."

Jack went into the kitchen – he still hadn't got used to the newness of it. His lunch was sitting on the formica worktop, beside the stainless-steel draining board. At least Jack assumed it was his lunch, for the parcel was carefully wrapped in the greaseproof paper of a plain loaf, and an elastic band round it. And the breadknife beside that, and the mangled remains of a white loaf in a pile of crumbs and broken corners of bread. He lifted the breadknife and shaved a few slices off the remains of the loaf for his breakfast. Back in the living room with his toast in his hand, Jack watched his father footering about with the fire.

"Yer ma'll kill ye if ye drap any food on the good carpet."

Jack laughed as a shower of crumbs fell onto the floor. It didn't feel like their own home yet, especially with no fire lit and both men hardly allowed to move.

The M'Cleans had been given an offer of a pensioners' cottage in the same estate, but with Jack's money coming in and him still wanting to live at home, they had enough points for a two-bedroom house.

"What time's yer bus? Are ye not late for yer work?"

"It's all right; it's my day for the Tech," Jack replied, but put his coat on and stuck his piece in his pocket anyway.

"See ye, da," he shouted as he pulled the front door closed with one finger through the shiny chrome knocker above the vertical letterbox.

It was cold and just getting light. Jack slowed his pace as soon as he turned out of Rosedown Gardens. The street lights were still on, right down the sweeping central spine road, alongside the Green, and on to the blaze of shop lights and roundabouts beside the community centre. He was in no hurry, but broke into a deliberate trot to keep warm till he got down to the shops where a few people were standing about near the bus shelter.

The only shop open was the newsagent's. Jack wandered in to scan the headlines on the papers without buying. Outside he took the elastic band from his piece and slipped it round his wrist. The rest went in the litter bin. There was no Tech, no job. Jack couldn't tell his ma he had left Ulidican just when they were flitting to Newbiggins. Not with her running round getting bits and pieces for the new house. As long as he left for work in the morning, and came back at night with his saved elastic band, no questions were asked. He never had to lie outright. There was the money, of course. Tuesday and Thursday mornings signing on at the Biroo. Between that and the fivers slipped to him for helping Dave Beggs out in his van, he always managed to have a tenner to put on the mantelpiece every Saturday morning. If he tried to hand it over direct, his ma would refuse it, no matter how badly it was needed. As it was, the money just quietly disappeared and Jack got two eggs in his Saturday morning fry.

Round at the end of the shops – the far end from the newsagents – was the door to the main concrete stairs. These took you up to the flats above the shops, three storeys of them, where Dave lived with his wife on the third floor.

Sally was from Northdyke Street and Dave from Fiji Street. They were just married and into the flat a couple of months, although they had been engaged for years. Jack remembered their engagement well, for that was how Dave owed him a favour. Two years back, Jack's ma had arrived up in his room early one Saturday morning. "Thon wee lad Beggs is at the dure for ye."

Jack pulled his jeans on and a pullover over his pyjama jacket.

"Bout ye, Davy. What's up?" Dave was white-faced.

"Jack, ye wudn't loan us twenty pound wud ye? A'm in desperate trouble."

Dave's da was a back-door frequenter of the Friesian Bull, and some connection of Hambo Jack's. Bugsy Beggs, as he was called, was either on the edge of criminal activity, or in the thick of it.

"Who do ye owe it til?" Jack asked. Judging by Dave's face, he had got into serious bother.

"A've to go wi' Sally to get the ring theday. An' A've lost the fifty pound we saved."

"How come ye lost it? Can ye not ask yer da?" Jack didn't know Dave all that well, so it was a bit strange he should come to try and touch him for money.

"Na, A lost everything on the horses last night. A'll never go in the bookies agane. An' Sally wud kill me. Please, Jack, A've already got thirty pound gathered up. A'll owe ye big time."

Jack took pity on him. He was actually shaking. It was worse than if he'd got mixed up with his da's activities.

"A've only a fiver. Wud that help ye?" Jack wasn't sure he was doing the right thing to hand it over, but the relief on Dave's face clinched it.

"Thanks, Jack, you're a real friend. A can pawn ma guitar, but you've saved ma life."

Recently, they had met up again in the dole queue on Jack's first day signing on.

"Are ye livin' round here now?" Dave asked. "Me an' Sally's got a wee flat above the shaps, in the Diamond. C'mon round after. How cum you're signin' on?"

"A toul' the Wetherals where to stick their oul job."

"Billie Jack! Good for you. What was it ye done there? Time an' Motion wi' oul tins o' food? That's a good one for signin' on wi'. There's not much call for them round here."

"What are you signed on as yerself?" Jack asked, curious to know what work, if any, Dave had been at.

"Fork lift truck driver."

An older man standing in front of Dave in the queue turned round. "I'm out o' work from 19 an' 53", he said with a wee smile.

"An' what's your line then?" Dave asked, hoping to pick up a few tips from an obvious old hand.

"A coronation programme seller," he laughed, as Dave sneered to Jack, "He's on his geg, so he is."

Dave's da had been set up as the proprietor of one of the two pubs in Newbiggins, The Buckie Gelder. Dave helped out cleaning up, and making deliveries in his da's van. Usually pubs had their drink and other stuff delivered to them, but Bugsy had other sources. And he supplied private parties and urban shibeens as well. And there was other work, like the mobile library, involving book runs between the Bigganreek Central Library and the Newbiggins Branch that had to be done in the official library van when it was available. The official mobile library driver was a friend of Bugsy's – or rather, he was a victim of the Buckie Gelder. Dave started doing Barney's runs for him as a favour when he was under the weather. Sometimes Barney came too, but sat in the passenger seat, sleeping. The Library staff at both ends turned a blind eye for Barney was only a year or two off retiring. Helping Dave out for regular handouts of cash was great for Jack. Never a dull moment, and the sense of freedom was elating.

As Jack climbed the concrete stairs to Dave's flat, he

wondered why anybody would put themselves through the sort of management training crap he had tholed at Ulidican.

Sally answered the door in her bare feet and a quilted dressing gown.

"Sshh!" She put her fingers across her lips and nodded him inside. "He's not up yet – away on in the sittin' room an A'll get ye a coffee." But she disappeared into the bedroom instead of the kitchen. Jack sat down on the settee and looked around the room full of electrical goods hardly out of their boxes. The plaster walls were bare, like his own had been when they moved. Cold, grey, smooth as glass and straight edges and sharp corners everywhere. They said you shouldn't paper the new finish-plaster, or paint it, till it dried out, maybe six months or more. Once you got past that wait, you forgot about it altogether.

Sally shuffled back across the living room into the kitchen with her slippers slopping and trailing like loose skis. "Take a feg, there Jack," she said. "The coffee's comin'."

Dave came in with a butt in his mouth, looking like death warmed up. "My lighter in here?" He lit up, squinted at Jack through the smoke, raised his skinny hand in a weak greeting and paddled into the kitchen after Sally.

"Last night too rough for ye Dave?" Jack shouted through.

"Sure he always looks that rough in the mornin's," Sally answered for him.

Dave came back in clutching his mug of coffee in one hand, his feg still blinding him.

"Well Jack," he said, "it's the Central Library first thing, to pick up some books and drop off some things at the boss's house."

"Oh, good," smiled Jack.

"A toul' ye," Dave said to Sally, "he fancies thon wee li-brarian, Bernie. She's a wee cracker, isn't she Jack?"

Jack didn't get a chance to answer, for Sally had an explosive temper.

"I'll cracker you, ye dirty baste ye," she said beating Dave round the head with a magazine. "I'll crack yer skull if ye pick up anything but books down there."

Jack presumed she had meant Dave wasn't to chat up any girls, not that she objected to them helping the Head Librarian out with a "homer."

The loading bay for the Big Library was down a side street from the main entrance. They had been there before and Jack knew the ropes. He jumped out and rang the bell beside the steel roller door. Suddenly it jerked into life and slowly lifted, revealing the Librarian from the feet up as he held the button. There only were four boxes of books and a bundle of post and papers for the branch.

"And you know my house, David?" asked the Librarian, "140 Cherryhill Road, up near the top. I need these two tall stepladders dropped off."

It was a bit of a sickener for Jack. Bernie had brought out the books and given them to Dave with a coy smile. She didn't look once at Jack. "And don't tell me the boss lives up near the Wetherals," he thought.

On the way back to Newbiggins Dave said, "We'll leave off the library van at the Buckie Gelder for Barney, and go back to the flat for lunch. Sally won't mind."

Sally didn't mind Jack coming back, but she was suspicious of Dave. He was a most unlikely lady's man – receding black hair and converging eyebrows. And he was as skinny as a rake with elbows and knees everywhere.

"What are you doin' home? Come in Jack. Well, you?"

"Just thought we'd come back for a bit o' dinner, seein' we were passin'."

"Did you get askin' thon wee girl at the library out, Jack?"

Jack looked at Dave before answering. Dave made all sorts of unscheduled "calls," and some of them involved dangerous liaisons, but surely not with Bernie?

"No, A didn't get speakin til her theday," Jack replied. But Sally had noticed the exchanged glances and glared at Dave.

"C'mon, love. Never min' Jack an' Bernie an' that. What about a wee quick bite?" Dave whinged, getting more suspicious-looking by the minute.

"A'll-give-ye-a-wee-bite-so-A-will." Sally punctuated each word with a blow to the back of Dave's cringing head and shoulders.

"Get aff, ye wee bitch." Dave lost his temper, but thought better of retaliating.

"C'mon, Jack, an' we'll get somethin' in the Buckie Gelder," he said, straightening himself up. "It's a bad job when ye can't get a feed in yer own house after an honest mornin's work."

"An honest mornin's work!" Sally shouted down the concrete stairs. "What's honest about doin' the double? Nathin'. An' see you, David Bloody Beggs, heaven help ye if ye're doin' the double on me an' all."

Despite her temper, Sally deserved better than Dave. Jack looked back as she watched them disappear down the concrete stairs with tears making her dark eyes shine. She forced a smile at Jack that seemed to say "I'm not blaming you now, Jack." His heart went out to her. She was much more good-looking than Dave. He didn't deserve her. Last night Jack had come back to Dave and Sally's from the Buckie Gelder, after dropping some of the lads off. With Dave snoring his head off on the settee, Sally made Jack a coffee and asked what happened him and Lily. "I knew her at school, ye know. Ye're better aff wi'out her. Sure she was always lukin' somethin' better. Never satisfied, her."

The Buckie Gelder was sad-looking in the middle of the

day. It was completely different from the Friesian Bull and all the other pubs on the Blackfort Road. For one thing it was enormous inside, like an airport departure lounge, with a wall-to-wall dark blue and red carpet. The bar in the corner was all glass and lights and mirrors. Among the optics was a "joke" clock that had numbers running round back-to-front, anticlockwise. One good thing about the clock, from Bugsy's point of view, was that when it was 10-to-closing time, it looked like 10-past to most of the customers. And there were the plaques – "Wanna Norwegian? Get a tonic tae," and "Oul Porters dinnae dee, the jist get carried aff." They were as jaded as most of the modern decor.

Scores of small round tables were dotted at random across the lounge, with short stools stacked upside down on top to allow the floor to be vacuumed. Beside the bar was a small platform where the entertainment happened. A glitzy gold drum-kit occupied the space, booking it for the evening's performance.

As Jack and Dave looked behind the empty bar counter, Bugsy emerged from the gents' toilet. It had a "Menfowk" sign on the door.

"C'mon th'ough to the pool-room an' get a toastit sam-wich," he said.

The only way for the public to get access to the pool-room was through the gents' toilet. This had the double advantage of keeping that inner sanctum for the use of men only, and to deter all but trusted, in-crowd regulars. The pool-room had a hatch into the back of the bar. From time to time ordinary customers might catch a glimpse of the pool-room when the hatch door opened, or of a glazed face appearing to get another round in.

Jack and Dave went to the back corner where a few grubby, upholstered chairs were arranged around a low rectangular table covered with cigarette burns. This part of the Buckie Gelder was more like the old-fashioned pubs of the Claw, right down to the sour smell of stale beer.

Last night the Buckie Gelder had been as it was meant to be, buzzing like a hive-full of bees. Jack had joined Dave in the lounge with the fill of five or six pulled-together tables. It was mostly the off-duty Newbiggins Protestant Boys Flute Band, with wives, girlfriends and flag-carriers. Unlike the bare walls of the pool-room, the walls of the big lounge were covered with coloured prints of old trams and horse-wagons. Hanging from the ceiling were four or five cart-wheel candelabras – electrified by white cables twisting conspicuously down the black chains holding them to the flat ceiling. Sally noticed that Jack seemed to be studying one of the pictures of a horse-drawn tram in Old Bigganreek.

"Ever been on one o' them, Jack?" she asked.

"No, but I remember my auntie takin me down the city centre on one of the oul 'lectric ones, before the trolley buses cum in, one Christmas." But that wasn't what was going through Jack's mind. Dave and his da had been on at him to join the Guild of Carriagemen. Bugsy had been a bus driver on the Blackfort Road, and then a lorry driver, until he started taking more interest in what had fallen off the back of lorries than driving stuff about. There was some connection between the themed decor of the Buckie Gelder and the "Truckers' Guild." Back in the pool-room a notice pinned above the bar hatch announced that the "Newbiggins Guild of Carriageworkers and Transport Hands meets in the Community Centre on the first Tuesday of the month at 7.30 pm." "Ask at the bar for further details," the notice ended. The immediate connection was that every first Tuesday of the month the off- duty Guilders met in the Buckie Gelder from half-nine.

Half the Newbiggins P.B.F.B. were in the Truckers' Guild, for although they were all born and bred in Auld Bigganreek, they weren't like their parents. The old timers kept going back to the Guild Halls in whatever parts of Bigganreek they had flitted from, and to the old guilds.

Newbiggins was a new start for everybody, and nobody felt it more than Jack. The lads in the Buckie Gelder had the same background as himself, but he couldn't have connected better to a crowd of mates if he had stayed in the Claw. As if to prove the point, half the rock group on the corner platform were in the Newbiggins P.B.F.B. too.

What did it matter if you couldn't hear what anybody was saying, when the cabaret was a rock band of your own mates? Cecil, the bass guitar player, was the most talented of the lot, although he had the least likely name under the sun for any budding pop star. Big Jim was a drummer and played with an equal strenuous, sweaty gusto for both bands. "Lockie" was passable on rhythm guitar and backing vocal. However, Norman Lockington's main contribution to the group was his girlfriend, Laura, the lead singer. Sally didn't care for Lockie at all. "See him, he loves himself, so he does," she said to Jack, pointing at him with her cigarette and tapping the ash off it with an emphatic forefinger. Dave's contribution to the group was to load their gear and drive them about in the van.

Jack ate his toasted sandwich and drank his pint standing quietly in the mid-day, day-after, quiet. Dave was out in the back checking what delivery runs were waiting.

"Is Lockie and Laura married?" Jack asked Bugsy, who just shrugged his shoulders and carried on wiping glasses, tables and empty ash trays with the same cloth. "I mean, when Dave an' me dropped them off last night he said to come round to their place if I wanted him to learn me the guitar."

Bugsie stopped dead. "Wud ye not be better learnin' to

drive the van, than lyin' about strummin' an oul guitar all day?"

Dave had just come in through the back door marked "Ootgang."

"Well," his da asked, "ye cud make a good trucker out o' him, cudn't ye?"

"Ay, but he's musical too ye know. Sure he cud learn drivin' an the guitar both, an mebbe have time for gettin' himself a wuman too." Dave gave Jack a knowing nod as his father stumped off, flicking his cloth at the legs of the pool table.

Jack drained his pint glass, noticing how much more mobile the remaining bubbles were on the empty glass of shandy than they always were with strong beer. He wasn't sure what Bugsy was getting at about him being made a Trucker. He never had much interest in the Guilds – certainly not the Fleshers and Fowlers. But then he hated everything to do with Ulidican, the Wetherals and the Ancient Craft of Food Processing.

Chapter 9

Systemic Culture

The new generation at Newbiggins could not be completely free of the Claw, not in their own time anyhow. And the old place was still back there, straggling on as a physical reminder to them all, even if it was now crippled by urban regeneration. For Jack there remained a tangle of roots – the band which had taught him all he knew about proper music; the tribal racing of his heart when he saw a guild parade; the innocence of childhood memories; a network of old friends and relatives; and, surging through it all, the pain and annoyance of being dumped by Lily. "Yinst bit, a lang whiles shy," as he learnt at school. The folk he didn't really like – and there were plenty of them – didn't matter any more, but, jings, he still detested the Wetherals and their likes. The Claw was still in his veins, like it or not.

The one friend from the old days he still kept in with was Reg Boucher, a flugel horn player out of Cherryhill Silver. Reg was married and living out of town in a chalet bungalow just beyond Newbiggins. He was for joining the Police Department once he got his exams, and the last thing he wanted to do was take over his father's butcher's shop in Northdyke Street. "A Boucher ownin' a buttcher's shap?" he would say. Even Jack slagged him off about his name: "'Bout ye, Boucher, oul mate, any oul buttcher's meat?" "Yeah, yeah," Reg would groan. Naturally enough, Reg was in the Fleshers and Fowlers Guild along with Jack. But as far back as Jack could remember, Reg only went out with the band when his Chapter wasn't parading too.

As long as Reg was prepared to call for him in his Morris Traveller and give him a lift to the band practices, Jack intended to stay in the silver band. But maybe not if Reg got into the Police Department Band. And only for concerts and contests, for if he joined the Trucker's Guild, he would want to parade with them rather than the band. He was forming new loyalties week by week.

Then on every other Saturday there was the home football match. Jack would still take himself on the bus to the Holy City and wait on the terrace corner for the old faithfuls to turn up. Half the Buckie Gelder crowd followed City too, so it might only be a matter of time before he would either stop going, or join the Buckie boys each match, right behind the goals.

The band, the football matches, and regular visits to relatives that still lived in the Claw, were the life-lines keeping Jack linked to his roots. Going back was a comfort blanket, a quilt of memories revisited for reassurance. But the fabric was frayed and fraying. Slowly but surely the connecting threads got weaker and weaker. If Jack had moved abroad, or if the M'Cleans had been the only ones to leave the Claw, its legacy would have disintegrated quickly. But Newbiggins was the Claw resettled in the suburbs. The collective memory had already taken root in its new setting.

"Is your auntie Betty still in Fiji Street?" Sally asked Jack when he sat down waiting for Dave to get dressed.

"Ay, why?"

"Oh, A was just wonderin'. She must be a fair age now. Dave's grannie's still a few doors up. He never bothers his arse goin' to see her any more."

"Oul Mrs. Beggs an' ma auntie's good friends. It's a pity o' the oul folks livin' there on their own now. A'm sure the' don't get looked after the same."

"Ye mean wi' everybody in an' out o' each other's houses? I used to hate that. But A suppose you go an' see her all the time?"

If that was a question, Jack left it unanswered. Dave had come in. Auntie Betty always wanted him to fill in forms for her, or go and do something for her that took half the day. Maybe when he had told his ma that he wasn't working any more, it would be safe to drop in during the week.

"Do the' still get their coal at Christmas – the pensioners?" Jack had seen a collecting box on the bar in the Buckie Gelder for the Pensioners Coal Fund, but he hadn't been sure if it was for the local old folks, or the Claw.

Dave joined in the conversation with a slight time lag. "What do you know about when I last seen grannie Beggs? Cherith keeps an eye on all the oul folks that's on their own."

"Who's Cherith then, when she's at home?" Sally was more interested in whether or not Dave was paying this new name any visits.

"Her an' Carla Jack runs the Corbie Centre, in M'Cabe's oul shoe shap."

"Ach. Is M'Cabe's shut down now? A suppose there's not the same pairs o' feet roun' there now." Sally was reassured that, whoever Cherith was, if she was along with big Carla, her Dave would be safe enough.

"Reg Boucher's for takin' me over to the Claw themorra night," Jack said, trying to keep the crack on safe ground. "If A've any time A'll drop in at Fiji Street maself."

Dave got up and put his City F.C. baseball cap on. It was blue with a black peak and the motto "Aye Ready" embroidered on in red stitches.

Not until they were outside did Dave tell Jack that they had to take the van over to the Claw that morning. "A wud'n plaise her," he explained. "She'd only think we were goin' because o' her naggin', so she wud."

They got in the van and were at the bottom end of the Claw in under the half-hour. A whole section up as far as Solomon Street had been flattened for redevelopment. Most of it was now rebuilt, but the whole street pattern had been changed. Quite tasty, like an architect's drawing come to life, wee trees and all. The Modern Irish Construction Association Housing contractors – MICAH – had a whole complex of temporary sheds and portable offices behind timber hoarding. Security was tight. There was little chance of Dave being involved in bringing or taking building materials. But as Jack sat in the van waiting for Dave to come out of the MICAH site office he was sure something was dodgy. And there weren't any girls in the site office, as far as he could see.

"Fancy a go at the wheel theday?" Dave said when he got back in and turned the key.

"Ay, what do ye mean but?"

"A'll take ye out along the five-mile straight whenever we're done."

"Dead on," Jack replied. This was the life.

The next stop was at the Corbie Centre, and Jack went inside with Dave.

"Hello stranger." A perky but slightly middle-aged Cherith greeted Dave with a look Jack was beginning to recognize.

They sat doon at yin o the scatter o tables in the front o the shop. It put Jack in mind o the youth club, wi'oot the teenagers. A wheen o yins were in an oot, in through the back and up and doon the stairs. Maist ignored the baith o them, but then in came Skipper M'Carroll. He stood wae his airms oot and a big grin.

"Billie Dave, what about ye, oul han'." As he said that, Skipper grabbed Dave's cap off his heid and beetled it wae his nieve into Dave's breist. "Bout ye, Jack," he added. "You're not in the Newbiggins mafia now too, are ye?"

Cherith brocht the three o them a coffee in roasting plastic cups.

"Wud Victor have left the snag list over from MICAH?" speired Dave at her.

"What's thon? Ye mean the things needin' fixed in the new houses?"

"Ay, Victor says he left it in here first thing."

Cherith gaed in the back to hae a look, wae a wee smirk and a "for you, dear, anything."

Whenever Cherith disappeared, Skipper cackled again and gien Dave another dig on the shoodher.

"What do ye think o' the way we done up the Centre?" quo he.

"Very good," said Dave, and Jack nodded too. There was a muckle great corbie paintit on the waa, wae a cherry scone in the yin claw and what looked like a string o puddings hanging frae the tither.

"A niver knew the' had sausages in them days," lauched Jack, for they kent the picture on the F & F Guild banner weel, – wae *The Prophet Elijah is fed by the Ravens* in siller letters unnerneath. "It's clever, but. A niver thought o' the Claw as a bird's claw."

"Who's payin' for all this then?" was Dave's speiring.

"The Residents Development Association, A mean, like, the Claw RDA, wi' a bit o' help from MICAH."

It was all abane boord, legitimate like. There wurnae onie

protection rackets involved, just a partnership – atween the residents and the developers. MICAH gien the people the hooses they wantit, the way they wantit them. After all, the residents were the customers, sae it was only richt that them that bigged the hooses should work alang wae, and support, the RDA. And that was where the snag list cum in. The Development Association made sure naebody jumped the queue for a new hoose, and they handled the after-sales-service. It was a bit like what the cooncillors and politicians used to dae. If ye had onie problems ava wae the new hoose, or things no working richt, it went on a "snag list" to MICAH, and what bits the RDA could sort oot, MICAH paid them for it. All abane boord, sae lang as the residents theirsels wurnae putting phantom snags on the list. And that's where Dave cum in. But Dave hadnae twigged that it was MICAH siller ahint the Corbie Centre and all.

"There's your grannie, Dave." Jack pointed wae his thumb towards a wee dumpy woman that had just rolled in the door.

"Ach David, son, are ye back? Have ye come to see us? Are ye waitin' here long?" There was nae space atween the speirings. No eneuch for onie lees, or onie answers ava.

"D'ye know Jack M'Clean, Betty's nephew?" Dave said, neatly passing the parcel.

"Son," Mrs. Beggs said to Dave, "the key's in the dure. Away roun' the lot o' ye to my house, an' I'll get Betty roun' for a wee surprise."

"Thanks, Miss Beggs, but A'm workin' – A've a wee job upstairs." Skipper was up and away afore the others could make onie repone.

Dave telt Jack to gang on ahead, he would catch up in the van afore he got to Fiji Street. He had to get the snag list frae Cherith, and hae a wee word wae her.

Back at grannie Beggs's, Dave was fidgeting to get away

mair nor Jack. Jack's auntie Betty was clearly nae stranger to Eadie Beggs's hoose. The pair o them were fechting in the working kitchen for control o the tay-pot.

"Don't be makin' any tay for us," Dave shouted in. But as Betty brocht in the tay, Eadie came in wae twa wee sherry glasses fu o broon lemonade.

"I know what our David likes. Do you like butter on yer digestive biscuits too, son?" she speired at Jack.

"I've a few messages to do down at the new houses," Dave announced, getting on his feet. "No, you stay here till A get back," he said to Jack wha went to get up anaa. "That's a' right isn't it, grannie?"

"Of course, son; we'll luk after him, won't we Betty?" The only yin it wasnae aa richt wae was Jack, but he was past caring if it came oot that he was on the Biroo. Anyhow, auntie Betty never listened, she just talked. She was much the same as Eadie, speiring a load o questions in a row, and then answering them hersel afore Jack could apen his mooth. She would hae been as much use as a Special Branch interrogator as a water-cannon at Waterloo.

"How come you're not at yer work theday? Have ye the day aff? Don't tell me you're on the Biroo as well? A suppose ye're givin' the men a haun out wi' the pensioners' deliveries? Ach, Dear love ye. Does yer mammie get free coal an' a Guild turkey at Christmas yit? Ye know yer man Brady from the builder's, Victor somebody the' call him. Ay, Victor Brady, he's a nice wee man, so he is, isn't he?"

"Na, who's he?" Jack said, showing he was taking tent o what his auntie was saying.

Victor Brady was the Association Housing Liaison Officer for MICAH. The mair the Residents Development Association did maist o the business, Brady liked checking oot for himsel that the residents were getting what they were due. Whiles a man frae the Ministry came wae him. It was hard telling whilk yin was checking oot the tither. In fact, Brady had called wae Mrs. Beggs that very forenoon, to see if there really was a flood in her back yard. Only somebody nice would take sic an interest, and only somebody big would come to the street door to see the back yard.

What a change frae the days Cooncillor Graham and the politicians gien oot the pensioners' coal, the Guild turkeys, the new hooses and got folks repairs done – the mair them things wurnae in their gift to gie oniehoo. The glory o gieing hand-oots o public siller back to the ordinary working man, where it all come frae in the first place, was nae langer a licht shining on the politicians. Their Constituency Clinics were run doon. And in gye bad shape ahint the coonter forbye. Jack never thocht aboot it tae he came back wae Dave til the thick o it. And what was wrang wae these changes? It maun be all for the guid, anyhow, these RDA shaps like the Corbie Centre. Mair power to the people's elbow.

Reg Boucher was aye sceptical, but. "There's no such a thing as Democracy," quo he. "Talk about Animal Farm!"

He maintained some o the heidyins o the Residents Development Associations would end up cooncillors themsels afore the century was oot. "Well, better them than the oul duffers that jist show their faces roun' the Claw when the're lukin' yer vote," thocht Jack. It was aye hard to tell wha was in it for themsels, an wha was in it for the people.

When Dave got back he wouldnae sit doon.

"Na, A've somebody out in the van, waitin' on us. C'mon Jack, better get back to it."

"When'll we see yis agane? Yis'll drap in before Christmas, now, won't ye?"

"Ay," he told his grannie, "we'll be back wi' yer coal, an' the turkey. Isn't that right, Jack?"

Jack shrugged his shoodhers and nodded as if to say, "Sure, that's all right with me."

As Jack was stepping out of grannie Beggs's, he stopped behind Dave wha was already at the door of the van. He had forgotten how yin step took you frae the inner warl o the Claw oot to the street proper.

"David!" His grannie cried him back in the hoose. "Don't be goin' wi'out the parcel for yer da."

Dave had to come back in past Jack to collect the broon paper bag. It had a half-dizzen o fresh scones in it, made while Betty was talking to her nephew. As Jack lent agin the door post, he looked up and doon the street, avoiding Cherith's smile from the van. At his feet, at the doorstep, was a scrubbed and bleached half moon o fitpad. It showed to the warl that a woman was in charge o the hoose behind it. A stranger had been at the door, for a cigarette butt was stamped oot on the half moon. Naebody frae the Claw would do such a thing.

They dropped Cherith aff at the end o Solomon Street, and went on up the Blackfort Road. An apen-sided coal lorry was making hard weather o the stye brae in front o them. It had coal bags stacked heich, but naethin held them on the lorry. Looking at the back o the truck put Jack in mind o the way they used to jump on the backs o lorries like thon at traffic lichts, for a free ride into toun. As they passed the end o Champion Street, Jack looked doon as far as he could see. Naethin much different there. "One last run and then home," said Dave.

A black arm wae a black hand at the end o it signalled oot o the coal lorry in front that it was turning richt, off the Blackfort Road. Not that it turning off would speed up Jack and Dave's journey onie, for Dave indicated richt and turned in after it. The lorry pulled into Bones's Coal Yard and they parked the van short o the entrance.

"We're not loadenin' any oul coal theday?" Jack groaned. "A have ma good workin' clothes on."

"Na, A'm just askin' when the Guild coals is gonna be ready."

Len Bones was vague. "The money's not th'ough yet," quo he. "I have to get it up front, then yis can come an' take it."

"Will it be bagged?"

"Depends," said Len, wi'oot explaining what it depended on. "An' where's yer mate from?"

"That's Jack M'Clean - from Champion Street, like."

After a short minute's thocht, as if he was going through the street directory in his heid, Len nodded, and turned on his heel.

Before getting back in the van, Dave walked back past it to a greengrocer's shop on the corner. He had spotted a bucket o daffodils on the outside stall marked doon to "Half-Price."

"For Sally," quo he.

"That's brave an' thoughtful," thocht Jack.

"Well, that was a waste o' time," Dave continued, talking aboot the visit to Len Bones. "An' it'll be a fat lot o' good goin' to the butcher's to see about the Guild turkeys."

"What butcher's is it does them? Is it still Boucher's on Northdyke Road?" Jack had it in mind to hae a word wae Reg on the way to the band themorra nicht. For all he knew, the war between the politicians and the RDA aboot wha was to gie oot the goodies to the pensioners and unemployed micht hae spread to the Christmas turkeys.

"Ay, sure it's yer own Guild does the collectin' for that, isn't it?" reponed Dave.

"But who delivers them now?"

"Us, lucky boy. An' we get well paid for it, so no slabberin', okay?"

"Is that right, but?" Jack speired, a bit concerned aboot

the morality o it all.

"Well if we weren't ye'd be unemployed and getting a turkey yerself – if ye'd rather have it."

If Dave and Jack were going to deliver coal and turkeys it was because the siller and the gear had been gathered by the Guilds. Was it no the Guilds that startit the custom? The Claw was a community that looked after its ain, nae matter what the process was. If ye didnae run it, ye damned it. That was yin lesson they had all learnt frae the heidyins o church and government.

"Sally'll get a quare gunk wi' you gettin' her flowers," said Jack as they climbed the concrete steps to Dave's place back in Newbiggins. When Jack saw the look on Sally's face, he made his apologies, and went on home.

"Where did ye get them?" he heard as he walked away.

"When A was up at the Corbie Centre – the' were half price," he added, wrongly assuming she was annoyed at him wasting money.

"Half price!" she echoed. "No wonder, for the're half dead."

"It's the thought that counts," he pleaded as Sally's anger rose in her.

"I know what ye're up to, ye – bloody – two – faced – git," she said, drumming the flowers on Dave's head till she was left with a handful of green stalks.

Jack saw a daffodil head pass him on the way down the stairs. It might make a good yarn in the Buckie Gelder, but he knew it was no laughing matter.

Reg Boucher was in bad form when he called for Jack to take him to the band. They didn't need their instruments as it was only a committee meeting in Sammy Dunlop's house. Reg was a brass band fanatic, and couldn't stand the thought of going to the band without getting a good blow. It was more the music he was into than the crack. Back when he lived in the

Claw he had an unrivalled collection of Championship Brass Band LPs – Black Dyke Mills, Fairy Foden Motor Works, CWS Manchester, you name it. Technically brilliant, but on a mono gramophone it never got your teeth vibrating. All Jack could remember of those LPs was the covers with full colour pictures of the bands in their trend-setting concert uniforms. Cherryhill only had marching uniforms with high, closed-up collars. At Reg's suggestion, at one earlier committee meeting, they went for self-supplied white jackets and bow ties for concerts and contests. And the Ladies Committee had made music-stand hangings for the entire band with the letters C.S.B. sewn on each one. It all made them stand out as a band with a touch of class.

The real cause of Reg being in bad form was the reason for the committee meeting they were heading to – a name change for the band. Sammy Dunlop, the band captain, and most of the rest of the band's hard core, wanted to change the registered name from "Cherryhill Silver Band" to the "James M'Carroll Memorial Silver Band." Jemmy M'Carroll had been Skipper's granda, shot dead by a sniper in the early troubles when the band was parading along Northdyke Road, towards the Mossvale Road. There had been no talk of a name change for 50 years, since then, and Skipper wasn't even in their band any more.

Reg's opposition to the name change was so strong it took Jack aback. "How did we get Cherryhill anyhow?" he asked Reg in the car. "Sure we never met on the Cherryhill Road, did we?"

"No. But the ban's first president was Lord Lowden o' Cherryhill Park, ye know, the original big house up there, like. And we never changed to Lord Lowden Memorial, did we?"

Jack knew that Lord Lowden had been a big noise in the Guilds too, for there was a clatter of them named after him, and even a Lord Lowden Orphan Schools Society – the L.L.O.S.S. fund which was one of the biggest Guild charities.

"A don't see what's the big difference in a name," he said, more as a question than an opinion.

"Well, if ye want the ban' to end up like any oul Kick-The-Pope ban', fair enough." After a minute's silence, Reg continued. "How d'ye think we get asked to lead the Guild Parade, or get hired by the respectable Guilds?"

It was a fact of life that factory "Works Bands" were unknown in Bigganreek. The captains of industry weren't going to be associated with bigotry in any shape or form. Without commercial sponsorship, their only source of funding was being hired for parades by the Guilds with plenty of money. And brass instruments cost a fortune. They gave up trying for Ministry money years ago. The captains of culture told them that their music wasn't a good enough standard for classical music support, and it wasn't eligible as traditional music because they played from written music. The real reason was that they were seen as cultural blasphemers that played marches and walked at the same time. It made good economic sense, what Reg was saying. But unless the young ones wanted to join the band, you would end up with plenty of instruments, and nobody to play them.

At Sammy's hoose, wae echt committee members perched roon the kitchen parlour, Reg got stuck in straight off. "When I joined the ban'," quo he, "it was the one place ye could get an instrument an' learn to read proper music. Luk at the worl' famous musicians that's cum up th'ough the ban's. Now the weans gets it all at school. Them Ministry boys is tryin' to squeeze all the good ban's out. Lord Lowden wud turn in his grave if he knew what the' were doin'."

Naebody spake agin Reg. They didnae want a row that would split the band.

"We'll take a vote," goes Sammy. "All them in favour o' stickin' wi' the oul name?" Only Reg raxed his hand up.

"An' who's on for the name change?"

Fower hands went straucht up, then Sammy's. Jack just shrugged his shoodhers in a gesture o abstentionism.

"Is that it then?" Reg speired, hardly fit to speak.

"Na, Reg, it has to go til the full ban', at the AGM. Houl on an' see what the rest think then."

Reg knew it was a lost cause. Jack felt sorry for him on the way back. But then Reg never went out with the band on parade anyway, for he was always with his own Guild Chapter. It was odd that he took it all so personally.

"I'll be joinin' the Police Department Band, anyroad," he said.

"Is the peelers hard to get into?" Jack asked, sensitive about his lack of support at the committee meeting.

"Why, ye interested?"

"A dunno; A might be."

Chapter 10

In Good Standing

If Jack wanted to get on as a driver, or a driver's mate, he would have to join the Carriagemen's Guild, and maybe even get his HGV licence. But first things first, and before he could transfer to the "Truckers" he would have to pay up any back dues he owed at the Fleshers and Fowlers. It needed one last visit, to lift his Prentice's Bond, and show he was a Guildsman in good standing. But even before all that, Jack had to get back into good standing at home. It was getting ridiculous, pretending that he still worked in Ulidican. And he couldn't join the Carriagemen's Guild without his da finding out.

It wasn't as hard as he thought. He just came out with it one tea-time.

"A'm not workin' in Wetheral's any more."

There were no looks of surprise, as if they already knew, and were glad he was being open and honest at last.

"Have ye got a new job?" Mrs M'Clean had been worried out of her mind – but not about the job. It was his strange behaviour, the way Jack seemed to be keeping even worse company than when he was going out with Lily Gamble. And he was coming and going at all hours. She was sure he would end up in trouble with the police.

"Well, not exactly, but if I can get my licence, I've been promised a start as a lorry-driver."

His mother couldn't think of any pit-falls in that. It must be well within the law if he was going to be licensed. A year ago and she would have been really annoyed at Jack giving up a good office job. But she hadn't the same neighbours to be proud at here in Newbiggins – and Jack was getting like a stranger in his own house.

"So," he continued, realising that the going was good, "A'll be leavin' the Fleshers an' Fowlers."

That was like a bombshell to John M'Clean. It was as if his son had announced he was changing his nationality, or giving up religion.

"What!" his da said. "What the hell's gates d'ye want to do that for?"

The relief was overwhelming when he learnt that Jack was only wanting to change Guilds, not renouncing King and Country.

And his mother was elated to learn that her son wasn't into drugs or mixed up with paramilitaries, or even worse. When the long-delayed confession was over, Jack was left wondering why he had left it so long. There was no inquisition or demand for any explanations. In fact, it cleared the air and replaced uneasy silences in the house with contented ones. Mrs M'Clean went down to the shops at the Diamond and bought in a packet of chocolate digestives along with her messages. She knew the packet would be finished as soon as it was opened, but that was what life was all about – enjoying the ups when they came.

Going back to the Fleshers Guild for the last time was not so easy. Reg called for Jack and talked the whole way over in his car about how he had lost interest in the band. They stopped at his father's shop on the Northdyke Road to give him a lift too, even though it was only a short dander.

"Ye leavin' us then, Jack?" quo he.

"Well, gettin' a transfer. Is the Carriagemen much different?"

"Same oul business. Sure there's none o' them the same nowadays. When I was your age there was hardly room for gettin' in. Sates two or th'ee deep roun' the Hall. An' hardly no room in the middle for workin' the degrees."

But that wasnae what Jack meant. As they speeled up the twisting, narrow stairs in the Guild Hall, Jack shivered. It was foundering ootside the actual rooms, even waur nor ootside proper. He could feel the coul on his face, radiating off the gloss-painted concrete walls. And he was a wee bit nervous getting, thinking o all the new nummers and words he micht hae to learn.

Inside the Chapter Room, used by a wheen o different Guilds, their ain banner was on poles leaning agin the wall o the stage. There was the familiar sicht o Elijah in lang white robes. Jack studied it for the last time. The auld prophet was sat sideways on, wae his heid turned so as you could see his white baird, and looking up (as he aye did) to the lift, where twathree corbies were bringing him his meal's meat. "*The Prophet Elijah is fed by the Ravens.*" And there were pictures o corbies and craas everywhere, being the emblem o the "Fleschers" (as it got spelt whiles).

Men were standing aboot in twas and threes, catching up on the crack, while the Ravenmaister was running about wae airmfu's o regalia, trying to get the show on the road. Jack was standing wae Reg when Ravenmaister Tommie Caldwell came up to them:

"You're liftin' yer Prentice Bond, thenight, aren't ye?"

"Ay, is there anything A got to do?"

"Have ye all yer dues squared up? Good. Then ye have to get tuk down a degree before ye can transfer. Ye know that don't ye?"

There were twa sorts o men there, auld boys like Cooncillor Tommy Caldwell and maistly wae baldy heids and broon suits, and young bucks like Skipper M'Carroll and his flare-leggit freens. Like oil and water, this generation gap couldnae be aisy blended into brethren, for they were sons and das at the end o the day.

Skipper was the Ravenmaister-in-waiting, and due to take ower frae Tommy Caldwell next summer. In the meanwhile, Tommy was going to show wha was boss. Ilka time Skipper made a mistake in the ritual, or stuttered ower his words, Tommy corrected him loudly and impatiently, even in the apening ceremony.

"What is the Guilder's first light?"

"The Book."

"The HOLY Book," snapped the Ravenmaister.

"Ay, The Holy Book," mumbled the Deputy Guildmaister, smirking like a naughty schoolboy, glancing at his cronies and winking.

"And where does it shine," growled Tommy.

"In the Chapter – A mean in THIS Chapter." There was a short gap as Tommy glared at his would-be successor, and drew in his breath slowly, as if considering whether to continue.

"Declare to the Guildsmen here present which Book and which Chapter contains our byordinar light."

"The Eleventh Book and the Seventeenth Chapter." The Ravenmaister then turned to Hugh Donaldson, the Senior Regulator.

"What do we find in that Book and that Chapter?"

"That the Ravens brung the Prophet Elijah bread an' flesh

in the forenoon, an' bread an' flesh in the evenin', an' he drunk from the burn."

Next to be addressed was the Junior Regulator, in truth the auldest man in the room.

"Why is that ancient light our code?"

"Because the Ravens, that had picked the bare bones … A mean, … picked bare the bones of every tribe, tuk no meat themselves till Elijah was fed and watered. For he had went into the wilderness at the call o' the Great Provider Above."

"So, as the Great Provider Abane sent the Ravens with meat for his servant, take 'CORVI VICTUM CARENT' for your watch and duty."

As the opening ritual ended, the guildsmen that wurnae speaking covered their mooths wae their left hands, and held out the "right hand of sustenance," as if offering food. The colours of the Fleshers and Fowlers were red and white, and all office holders wore white gloves with red slip-on cuffs. A black corbie's wing was painted on each cuff.

Jack pree'd all this gear for the last time. A wooden boord wae all sorts o symbols charted on it hung on the side wall. The muckle corbie painted in the middle had the Guild's watchwords in Latin underneath: "Corvi victum carent." There was something gripped in the Corbie's claw that aye put Jack in mind o the American eagle wae a fistfu o arrows. The Latin motto had a matching abbreviation "C.V.C." and a translation along the bottom o the boord – "Ravens do without food." Maist folk, Jack included, had aye thocht it meant "The Corbie carries the Victory."

The "dropping" degree that Jack was gart gang through was like a backwards running o the "Corbie-Craa" degree, yin he had seen many times before. But you cannae take the secrets oot o somebody – just lock them away solemn-like.

"Drap us off at the Buckie Gelder," Jack said to Reg on

the road back from the Chapter. There was still an hour or two to go before closing time.

"Ye comin' in yerself?" he said as they turned in past the shops in the Diamond.

Dave and the lads were well oiled by the time they came in. Reg was a bit uncomfortable with all the racket and boisterousness.

"Boul Jack, …" The rest of Dave's greeting was drowned out by the boys banging bottles on the tables and singing, "We are, We are, We are the billie Boys …"

"Is that you done wi' the Fleshers now?" Dave guldered, spraying a mist of reaming nappy in Jack's face as he spoke. Jack nodded. "Right, we'll get ye in wi' us next Chapter meetin'. Right lads?"

Reg made his apologies and left without getting a drink for anyone in return.

"Who's thon bundle o' laughs?" Dave took exception to Reg's obvious haste to get away.

"Reg? Oh, he's a mate o' mine from the band – he's thinkin' o' joinin' the police."

"Just luks like a peeler, so he does."

Jack had stopped being invited back to Dave's after the "Buckie" shut up shop at night. The argy-bargies between Sally and Dave were getting worse and the stony silences worse again. Not only had Sally stopped coming down to the pub with Dave, but she started to have her mother round at nights, or she would go into town to visit Dave's grannie herself.

Then even that stopped. It wasn't the drink that was burning up all Dave's money. It was his old taste for the bookies. He could go for weeks without a bet, but once he went in, he just couldn't stop until he was cleaned out. Once the money was finished, the bits and pieces in the flat started to go too, and even the housekeeping. The odd thing was, he drank in a crowd but betted as a complete loner. Only Sally knew how bad things were getting, not even Jack.

"A can't have my own mother roun' any more," was a frequent girn.

When Jack called in the mornings, Dave was usually ready, or asked him to wait at the door if he wasn't.

"Come in, Jack," Sally said one morning. Obviously something was up. The place was like a tip, and no sign of Dave.

She eyeballed Jack to show there weren't tears in her eyes, but she was shaking.

"Has he left?"

"No," said Sally. "It's his grannie. He's had to go over to see her. She's not well."

Dave was shaking when he let himsel into his grannie's hoose. It was the peep o day in Fiji Street. A few neighbour-women had the fire lit and were sat at it.

"She won't get out of her bed till she sees you, son."

Dave went to the back scullery. His grannie's bed had been put there frae the stairs had got too much for her.

"What's wrong, grannie?"

"Ach, son, A'm just done. Would ye sen' for the doctor?"

Mrs Beggs had never been to see a doctor, for she didnae believe in them.

"Betty, ye wouldn't know where to get a doctor for grannie, wud ye?" he said when he returned to the kitchen parlour.

"Oh, I'll go. I'll go, son. You stap here."

The doctor was in wae her for nae mair nor twa minutes tae he came back oot and sent for an ambulance. Straucht off she went, wae Dave in the back alang wae her. "This is it son," she said. "I won't be comin' out."

Dave never had to cope with anything like this before. "Catch yerself on, grannie, ye'll be all right."

"Don't you worry, David. I'm just ready to go when the Lord calls." There was nae answer to that.

It was hard to believe, as she lay wae her een fast shut on the ward bed, that this was the wee woman that waited at the school gates for Dave when he was a wean. She would hae taen him roon to her hoose for "his favourites" – digestive biscuits wae butter on them. They were only his favourites because his grannie aye told him they were.

"Would she be in pain, Nurse?" Sally asked frae the other side of the bed. The nurse reached over and squeezed grannie Beggs's ear. She didnae budge.

This dying thing was new to baith Dave and Sally. At the funeral the plain-clothes preacher hit the lot o them up the bake wae the Gospel Truth.

"Look after Sally, thon wee wife o' yours." How many times had Dave heard that frae his grannie? And, "Would ye not give yer grannie a visit?" How many times had he heard that frae Sally?

Damn the hair! It was down to the Buckie Gelder to drown the guilt.

Sally hoped all Dave's religion hadn't been buried with his grannie. But it wasn't his soul she wanted to save. It was her own marriage, or at least salvage some sort of a life. Money or the lack of it was the root of the problem. Annie Kavanagh and Ruth from Samoa Street had both been at the funeral. They had promised to come and see Sally in her new house some time. "D'ye remember school?" Ruth had said. "We'll have a good oul chin wag."

"Come up any night. Dave's always out, so there'll just be me.

True to her word, Ruth made the journey. But she could see straight away that something was up with Sally … and Dave.

"I think I'm goin' to crack up," Sally confided in Ruth,

even though she hadn't seen her for years – and had never been really friendly with her anyway.

"Sally, ye know what the answer to all yer problems is?"

"Ay, a sugar-daddy, or findin' buried treasure." She avoided saying "winning the pools," for trying to do just that was at the heart of the problem.

"Jesus," said Ruth.

"What?"

"Do you want me to pray for ye?"

"Oh! – Ay, … thanks Ruth … that would be very good o' ye." Sally was wounded by that. It was Dave that needed saved, and prayed for, and that.

Joining the Newbiggins Guild of Carriagemen was a novelty for Jack in more ways than one. The Book and Chapter numbers were different – Seven and Eighteen – as you would expect, but the opening was much the same. Of course, there wasn't a Raven in sight, and the byordinar light had no obvious meaning: *So the Danites turned and set out from Micah at Mount Ephraim with the weans and kye and the carriage before them.*

The modern room in the community centre with its large, curtained windows left little space for the clutter of old pictures and wall charts Jack was used to in the old Guild Hall. Dave and the rest, young and old, were bedecked in green and silver regalia – collarettes, aprons, and officers' capes. The guild colours of green and silver were in an alternating wedge pattern on the collarettes. Very different, the total effect, to that of the assembled Fleshers with their plain red regalia edged with a simple white border.

The banner, mounted in the usual place, was the "back" side – a picture of silver-armoured biblical soldiers overlooking a green wooded landscape. A mountain in the background looked remarkably like the Clinty Brae that towered over

Bigganreek. The legend across the bottom of the picture read, "*The planting of Laish by the Danites*." Whether it was the planting of the trees or the Danites themselves, it didn't matter, for there wasn't much action there. Jack was more familiar with the "front" side of the banner, the one you saw coming at you on parade. That was a picture of Samson pulling the columns of what looked like Bigganreek City Hall down round him. But the Danites moving into Laish was how the Carriagemen saw themselves every time they walked behind their banner, from the start of the parade to the finish.

Having lifted his Prentice Bond from the Fleshers, Jack only needed to go through the "Carriage" degree to complete the transfer. The enactment of this alternative scene of Biblical folk drama was not completely destroyed by its modern setting.

Jack was taken as a captured Levite priest to the house of Micah at Mount Ephraim. Here he was to officiate at the melting down of 600 shekels of silver to make a number of graven "silver" charms and a casting of a false god. But five Danite spies arrived at Mount Ephraim from the coastal lands round Joppa, looking for more land to inhabit.

"The nearby Land of Laish," Jack was told to advise them.

"In whose name do you speak?" he was asked by the Carriagemaister.

All Jack's responses were then given by a wiry wee man with a long staff, acting as his guide.

"He speaks in the name of the Great Mover, who has carried him here to the house of Micah."

"From where were you taken?"

"From Bethlehem in Judea."

"Why were you taken?"

"As one of the priestly tribe of Levi, to be an idolatrous priest to Micah."

The five Danite spies withdrew and came back with six Danite "centurions."

"Where is the land that has been chosen for us?" they demanded.

"Laish," Jack's guide replied.

"Will you stay at Mount Ephraim, in the house of Micah, or come with us and be our priest?"

Jack was told to make his decision either to go with the Danites and plant in Laish, or to stay with Micah and his household. The centurions had a large green sheet, nearly the size of the banner, which they held flat, so that it carried 600 pieces of silver, about the size and shape of milk bottle tops. This sheet was the carriage on which they threw all the graven and cast silver images from the house of Micah.

"If ye'r joinin' us, put the silver images in the carriage an' follae it." The men carried the green sheet loaded with silver to the far end of the hall and laid it on the floor. After it was spread out and each man put one foot on the green sheet, Jack was escorted right onto it.

"As the Levite priest was carried off to this new land so the carriage also contained the abused 600 pieces of Micah's silver."

Jack's mind was wandering. Although he was the centre of attention, he nearly forgot where he was, till he heard the voice of one of the other men. He came back with a start, not sure if he was being asked a question.

"See how you have arrived, driving the carriage before you, in a land of plenty."

Jack looked round him and nodded, hoping he wasn't expected to say anything.

"See the silver. It represents the inheritance won for you an' entrusted til ye. If you abuse it, or carry it aff for your own use, or make a false god o it, then you forfeit the right to your inheritance. Both here and hereafter."

"The carriage must be your brother's load. No weight will bog you down like the burden o' your own possessions."

There was no way Jack took all that in, no matter how solemnly he swore to it. His mind wandered here and there. The words were like mercury bouncing off paper, but the pageant of sights and actions stuck in his mind like indelible ink. It was much the same with the final reading of the story from the Holy Book. The actual passage tied in with the ritual all right, but it was the unauthorised use of the Ullans Version, rather than the King James's one, that took him aback. They never used the Ullans Bible back in the Fleshers. In fact, he was sure he had been told that the Honourable the Grand Society of Guild Companies (the Hammermen) had ruled out the use of anything but the Authorised Version. Not that any of the Guilds took notice of new rulings from the Hammermen any more.

The strangeness of the sound of the reading registered strongly with Jack, rather than its content. It was easier to follow than the King James when it was read out. But it was a rare enough occasion to hear it, for the Ullans Bible wasn't used in proper churches.

Dave's Uncle Nigel, who was a bus driver when not imagining himself in the Promised Land, did the reading:

In thaim days, the wur nae käng ower Israel, an in thaim days tha Tribe o Dan socht thairsels a heirskip o lann fur leevin in; fur tae thon day a heirskip o thair ain hadnae fell tae thaim amang tha tribes o Israel.

An tha childer o Dan ootpit frae thair fowk five men frae thair shores, men o sowl, frae Zorah, an frae Eshtaol, fur seekin tha lann an sussin it oot; an the telt thaim, Gang, pree the lann; quha, quhaniver the cum til Ephie's Moontain, til tha hoose o

Micah thar, the taen lodgins oot.

Quhan the wur ootby tha hoose o Micah, the heerd tha tongue o tha callan Levite an kent it; an the gaed ben an axed him: Quha brocht ye here? An quhit wud ye be daein here?

An he telt thaim, This road an thon Micah haes truck wi me, an A'm his preest.

An the sayed til him, Ye wudnae hae a wurd wi God, wud ye, an ax quhit gate we maun gang fur tae wun guid an fouthie.

An tha preest telt thaim. Gang wi lown: afore tha Loard bis tha gate ye maun gang.

Syne tha five men set oot an come til Laish, an seen tha fowk at bidet thar, quhit-wye the leeved tentless-like, efther tha wyes o tha Zidonians, queet an siccar; an thar wus nae Jaw Pee's in tha lann, at micht pit thaim tae shame in ocht; an the wur far frae tha Zidonians, an haed nae truck wi onie man.

An the cum til thair brithern bak at Zorah an Eshtaol: an thair brithern sayed til thaim, Quhit hae yis tae say?

An the telt thaim. Get yersels riz fur gangin agin thaim; fur we hae seen tha lann, an, hae, it daes he gye an guid: an quhit- wye ir youse? Dinnae be sweir o flittin an takin tha lann.

Quhan yis gang, ye'll cum on a fowk at's siccar, an til a big kintra: fur God haes gien it ower til yer hann; a lann quhaur thar bisnae want o ocht ava in tha hale yird.

An thar gaed frae Zorah an oot o Eshtaol säx hunner men o tha Tribe o Dan bearin airms o war.

An the gaed up, an made an encampin in Kirjath-jearin, in Judah; at's quhy-fur the caa thon pairt Mahaneh-dan til theday: see, hae, it's ahint Kirjath-jearin.

An the gaed up tae Ephie's Moontain, an cum tae tha hoose o Micah.

Syne tha five men as haed tha lann spyed oot reponed, an telt thair brithern, Dae yis ken at ben thon hoose is a preest's simmit caa'd an ephod, an siller chairms, an a siller graven image, an an idol castit wi meltit siller forbye? Sae noo tak tent o quhit ye maun dae.

An the turned aboot an cum til tha hoose o tha Levite callan, at wus tha hoose o Micah anaa, an salutit him.

An tha säx hunner men o tha Tribe o Dan wuz at tha inlat o that yett, stuid stannin wi thair weapons o war.

An tha five men as had the lann spyed oot gaed up an cum in ben, an taen tha graven image, an tha ephod, an the chairms, an tha castit idol; an tha preest wus in tha inlat o tha yett stuid wi the säx hunner men at haed tha weapons o war.

An thaimyins gaed ben Micah's hoose an brung tha graven image, tha ephod, an tha chairms, an tha castit idol. Syne tha priest spiered o thaim. Quhit ir ye at?

An the telt him. Houl yer lown, pit yer haun ower yer mooth, an gang wi iz, an tae iz be a faither an a preest: wud it no be bettèr fur ye bein a preest til a tribe an familie o Israel?

An the preest's hairt wus blythe, an he taen tha ephod, an the chairms an tha graven image, in tae tha mdddle o tha fowk.

Sae the turnt an set off an pit tha weans an tha kye an tha carriage afore thaim.

The big difference, thought Jack, was that the Fleshers were about sharing out provisions, while the Carriagemen were about trafficking money and land.

"Ay, but it's what ye're supposed to do wi' it when you get it," Dave said as they walked the short distance across to the Buckie Gelder. "Talkin' of which, A'm out o' money for a pint. Anyhow, Sally sez for us to come up after, if ye want."

Jack gave him a look to see if he was serious. He was. It was nothing new for Dave to be out of money, but to be welcome back at the flat was something he had not experienced for months.

The minute they arrived at the door, it was clear there was

a buzz in the place. "I've a wee surprise for ye, Jack. Look who's here." It was a smiling, sparkling Ruth, who was as much a surprise to Dave as to Jack. She was oozing warmth and excitement, and all directed at Jack. Was this a sort of a blind date? He couldn't take the idea of going out with her seriously, not with her being friends with Lily and still living in the same street and all.

"Did you get on all right at the Chapter, boys? I never miss them when they're walkin'. A love to see the men out wi' the Guilds. Do you not, Sally?" She was all chat, Ruth.

The flat was prepared as if for a church daffodil tea, with wee fancy sandwiches and sausage rolls on plates here and there. "Do you want tea or coffee, Jack?" she gushed.

"Oh, coffee."

"De–DAAHH!" And in from the kitchen walked a tray held by a very embarrassed Lily Gamble!

Talk about stilted conversation! But Ruth was in her element. "Lily, tell Jack about this," and "Jack, tell Lily about that." There was no way Jack and Lily could converse, even politely, with such intensity observing their every word. To their relief, the night turned into a "discussion" on the rights and wrongs of the Carriagemen's Guild, with Ruth acting as convenor. It was a daft sort of a night, but with Jack trying to hide the fact that the only thing he wanted to know was why Lily was there. If Lily was to leave early by herself, then he could ask Ruth, or Sally. Or maybe he would get a chance to talk to Lily later, by herself. Anyway, it was in the lap of the gods, or of Ruth.

"Isn't it awful the way some Guildsmen don't live up to their promises?" Ruth gave out her starters for ten.

"What man o' any sort does?" Sally said with a jag. Fortunately for her, Lily laughed and Dave took it as a joke.

"A mean, about money. That's not what makes ye happy,

is it?" said Ruth persistently.

"Well it doesn't make ye happy bein' skint," Dave said.

"It's not havin' it that's wrong, it's wantin' it that bad ye'd rob and cheat to get it."

Sally nodded her head in agreement. "Ay, an' …," but she stopped as Dave got stuck in.

"A suppose you think the people in the Bible should have stayed put in Egypt, an' not got out wi' all the pruck the' cud find?" Jack smiled. He knew Dave had Ruth there.

"An' what about the Danites?" Jack said, but Dave gave him a look and held up his hand as if he was about to give away Guild secrets. "Or us here in Ulster, an' in America," he continued, changing track slightly. "D'ye think we should give everything back to the natives?"

"It wud be a hard job," Lily laughed. "Sure they're all dead hundreds o' years."

"No, I don't," Ruth said, seriously. "I think it's all part of God's plan. But it's wrong to take what we've been given an' make out it's just for ourselves."

"We weren't given it." Dave was getting annoyed at Ruth, who seemed to be getting personal. "We had to fight for it."

"I suppose you think as long as you can get off with it, you can take what ye want?"

"Ay, why not? D'ye think the pagans were just for handin' everything over because it was God's plan?"

No matter what advice Ruth was giving her, it didn't seem to help Sally to get on any better with Dave. The rows got worse and worse, and each time things were cast up, Dave would get a "Ruth says …" That only confirmed his suspicion that Sally was confessing all his sins to her.

"Money, money. That's all you slabber on about." Dave had had enough of her whinging and nagging. She never complained when he had a wee win at the dogs, providing he managed to win it on the last race and came straight home.

The next Saturday morning Dave was heading out.

"Ye goin' to the match?"

"No."

"Where are ye goin' then?"

"Out."

"Out where?"

"Outside."

Sally grabbed her coat in a flailing temper and, slamming every door within reach, stormed out of the flat. Her coat whipped angrily against the door post, with buttons cracking. Dave caught up with her and grabbed her by the arm.

"Where are you off to, then?"

"Out-bloody-side too."

Dave said, "Calm down, love. Tell ye what. D'ye want to go across town to the Waterside Park for a dander?"

The idea of going for a walk in the Park on a cold Saturday morning didn't really appeal to Sally, but they did need to talk, and that was where they had done a bit of their courting. It just might re-jig those days of pre-marital social intercourse, when they could, and actually did, talk.

They walked through the gates, down to the side of the muddy water, past banks of boring old shrubs with litter stuck in the bottom branches. It was all silence. "Well?" Sally said eventually. "I thought ye wanted to talk? So talk."

"It takes two to talk. What d'ye want to talk about?"

"I'll tell ye what. Why can't ye open yer mouth without talkin' about yerself an' what you want? When did ye last …?" It was all downhill from there. Dave just let her rabbit on. By the time they got to the gates at the other end of the Park, Dave had suffered in silence as much as he could take. There was a bookies on the other side of the street.

"Wait here. Just one minute. A won't be more than a

minute. A want to catch the 10.30.”

Sally stood shivering in the cold outside the bookies for five or ten minutes. Just as she was about to walk off, Dave came out. “Told ye A wudn’t be long, so A did.”

“What are you lookin’ so pleased about?”

“My wee pony came in at 7 to 1. If A’d more than two pound to put on her we’d be flyin’.”

“An how long will ye houl’ on to that?”

As they walked back through the Park, they started rowing again. One minute Dave was guidering at Sally and she was looking straight ahead like thunder. The next she was screaming at him with Dave fit to explode.

Then they both started at the same time, shouting, stopping, walking back and forwards at each other, pointing, until Sally put her hands on her hips and said, “See our marriage. It’s pointless. It’s makin’ the both o’ us oul before our time. We might as well pack it in …”

Dave said nothing, and they walked on with Sally holding her face in her hands, sobbing. They were nearly back at the Park gates.

“Maybe ye’re right. If ye want to call it a day …” Before they could finish their conversation, Sally turned off the path. “I’m away in here to the Ladies,” she said suddenly, biting her bottom lip.

It was Dave’s turn to wait, shivering. He supposed he was supposed to wait. He walked up and down a bit, cooling off, literally. It was freezing. And he waited.

Still Sally didn’t come out. Still he waited. All sorts of things started to go through his mind. Maybe she had done something stupid like slashing her wrists or taking all the pills she was on for her nerves, in the one go.

After another desperate wait, Dave went over to the buffer wall at the entrance to the Ladies. He was about to shout

"Sally, are ye all right?" when he heard the sound of somebody coming out.

"About time," he was going to say when a strange middle-aged woman came out, glared at him and walked past him quickly as if he was a pervert. Still he waited. Still no Sally.

Maybe she could see him from inside, and wasn't going to come out until he went away. As long as she was all right. But he couldn't leave until he found out.

Eventually, Sally emerged both crying and smiling. "What kept ye? What's up?" Dave couldn't understand her big broad smile. She must have found money or a purse or something in there, he thought. Well, that would be a turn up for the books.

"Sally," he said, "what's the score? Did you find a purse in there or somethin'?"

Sally looked at him in a way he hadn't seen before. "No, Dave, but I did find the Saviour."

Dave was just about as dumbfounded as he would have been if she'd staggered out covered in blood. He pointed stupidly towards the door. "In thonner?" he asked, not sure he had heard her right.

"In here," Sally replied, and tapped her chest, before starting to walk on out of the gates back in the direction of home. Dave trotted after her.

"Ruth has been talkin' to me about the Lord," Sally began to explain.

"An' prayin', A suppose," Dave said sarcastically.

"Yes, prayin'. She told me that Jesus died for ordinary folk like me an' her. An' it wasn't just like them that died for us in the war, or in the RUC or that."

There was something robotic in the way Sally was talking. "What's the difference?" he asked. But it wasn't intended as a question.

Sally went on. "For they're dead an' gone an' never knew

us. He's still alive but, an' knows me for maself. Ruth said I would know when the time came an' I needed to come to Him. In thonner A just come to the point where A give ma whole life til Him."

Dave didn't like the sound of all this. She must have cracked up completely. And he might just be to blame. Hopefully, if he was patient, she would get back to normal.

But over the next days and weeks, Sally stuck to it. Dave tried provoking her, almost longing for her to lash out at him, but she just answered "Yea?" or "Maybe you're right, Dave."

Now it was Dave's turn to go on at Sally. He couldn't bring his friends home any more, in case they got the same treatment. How could you cope with this? It was like having a mad aunt locked in a back room. After about a fortnight, Dave decided a different tack was necessary. He was stretched full out along the settee when Sally came in from the shops with a cheery smile on her face.

"D'ye know what has happened wi' you, Sally?" he asked. He continued without waiting to be prompted. "Your nerves is gone. Ye've turned to religion for a way out. Some folk go on the drink, but you've just gone religious. Don't go over the top now. It's just yer nerves."

"Oh, ay!" she said, confronting him with "that" smile. "It's my nerves is it? You're somebody to talk. Just luk at yerself. The nails is chewed off ye, smokin' sixty a day …" She walked on into the kitchen, turning in the door to have the last word. "You just think about it an' ask yerself, whose nerves is away wi' it, yours or mine?"

Chapter 11

Nappies and NIPD Blues

Annie Kavanagh's babbie was just twa month auld when he gien his first big goofy smile. He wasnae a "bonny baby," for he looked ower much like his granda, Cooncillor Graham, for that. But the neighbours all thocht he was a "lovely wee ba." Annie was fit tae burst she was that proud.

"Bobby, my wee Pride o' the Claw," she aye called him.

"Wud ye stop callin' him that," Paul kept saying. "That's the name o' a ban'." As Paul was band secretary o the Claw Defenders F.B., he was gye defensive got aboot losing members, or parade bookings, to the "Pride." Annie's mother had just aboot moved in with them. "My wee Annie needs luked after for a week or two," she told her husband as soon as Annie got hame frae the hospital. Twa month on and she was still there, fower or five nichts a week.

Eric Bates's auld hoose, after a honeymoon period wae the young Kavanaghs, was noo apen hoose for yin and aa. Annie's bairn was a big draw. Even Mrs Graham aye being present didnae put the neighbours aff. Forbye, there was no way the combined effect o the new ba, the obsessed ma, and the resident guid-mother was for putting Paul oot o his ain hame. Annie's friends, like Ruth and Lily, were in and oot all the time. And when they were in they were all in!

"Away, Paul, up the stairs and practise the flute or somethin' till we have a bit o' girl talk," said Ruth.

"Ye will not! Ye'll wake the wean," chorused the combined instincts o mither and ma-in-law. There was a sort o maternal domino effect there, brocht aboot wae the bairn's hame-coming.

"Why don't ye go up to my house?" said Lily. "Billy's in."

The minute Paul went oot the door, Annie started.

"Well, tell us all about it. Did ye see Jack? C'mon Lily —." Maist conversations in the hoose were steered roon tae wee Bobby, or tae the great crack it was in the hospital wae the other mithers. Annie wusnae fit for yin-track conversation-steering, the way Ruth was wae religion. Anyhow, in this case, the diversion o Ruth and Lily's visit to Newbiggins was compelling.

"He hasn't changed one bit."

"But, did yis get thegither agane?"

"Not at all. Sure we just went over to see poor Sally."

"Oh ay, pull the other one."

Ruth turned to Lily hersel and speired, "Would ye not go out wi' him agane, then – if he ast ye like?"

"A don't think so. There's not really anythin' there. It was good seein' him but. Just as a friend, like, ye know."

"Sally's gettin' on great an' all," said Ruth. "She's like a new person."

"Any talk o' her an' Dave startin' a family?" countered Annie.

"A can't see it," said Lily.

Things in Samoa Street had quietened down richtly frae all the trouble that afternoon. Paul had come back frae the fitbaa match and said there had been a bit o trouble after. Some o the city supporters had tried to get into the Mossvale Road until they were stopped by the polis. And then they turned on them.

While they were at their tea, door-to-door rumours were spreading that a Mossvale mob were rioting, and had got onto the Blackfort Road. Annie panicked. First thing was she started darting back and forrits in the hoose, and then ootbye, like a chicken gien a powerfu scare at the sicht o a fox. Then she was oot on the Blackfort Road looking away doon tae where the commotion was. It was near oot o sicht.

"What are ye doin', just standin' here?" quo she to this peeler stood at the end o Samoa Street. "I've a wee baby in the house. Get away down there and do your job."

"You just go back in your house and do your job, an' I'll do mine," the policeman snapped.

After the girls had left Annie's, Paul came back in.

"Do you know the museum the've opened in Cherryhill House?" he speired at his mother-in-law. He had nae form o address for her. "Mrs Graham" would make it soond as if he wasnae boss in his ain hoose.

"Ay, why sure my Jim opened it. Why d'ye want to know?"

"Lily's ma was talkin' about it. She says she'd like some-body to take her up an' see it. She thinks she has some sort o' connection wi' it. Photos or somethin'."

Mrs Graham got a bit prickly aboot the subject o the museum.

"Why don't ye ask some o' yer friends down at the Corbie centre? Sure hasn't ones from the Development Association got jobs up there?"

Cooncillor Graham and his wife hadnae been back to the

museum at Cherryhill House frae it apened. At the opening, the Minister of Culture told the press that the display would be a fitting tribute to the prominent role the Lowden family had played in the growth o Bigganreek, in all aspects of its commercial and political life. The beautiful house and demesne itself, gifted to the nation, would be a real attraction too, of course. But fowk were mair interested in Lord Lowden's Guilds, and life in the factories, than in his role in setting either up. And maist o all, there was thon tremendous collection o auld photographs of Bigganreek in the olden days. Cooncillor Graham couldnae thole the sleekit way some o the staff at the museum (maistly them that had got their jobs through the Claw Development Association) had turned it intae a People's Museum. Noo it was concerned wae the ordinary folk o the Claw. And they kept on changing it, the mair o all the undertakings gien to cooncillors by the men frae the Ministry. "People are voting with their feet – visitor figures you know. If people aren't interested in what we exhibit, then it'll just have to close." That's what they were saying now.

"I know why Mrs Gamble wants to see it," Annie's mother said. "Her father, a lovely man, in the Total Abstinence Guild, was in the fire brigade you know. Never walked in the Guilds for he was crippled. Ye see, he fell through the roof at a big fire in Cherryhill House. Lord Lowden got him a job after in Thompson's Toffee Factory. I think he half owned it, or had shares in it or somethin'. Anyhow, when we were at school, Lady Lowden would be doin' her visits an' would always ask to see the fireman's children. Lily's mother was in my class at school, you know. Lovely woman. Lady Lowden, I mean."

Annie got up for the tenth time in as many minutes to check the babbie. This time Paul followed her and grabbed her from behind, squeezing her.

"What about an early night, thenight?" quo he.

"Get aff, are you on yer geg? D'ye not think ye've done enough damage wi' thon thing?"

He came back into the kitchen parlour wae his mind back on the subject.

"Ay, she said she'd like to see if there was any oul photos o' folk she knew."

Spring in Newbiggins was a long time a-coming. Sally might have got herself a new life, but for Dave the winter seemed as if it would never end. It was a dour, dismal winter of tracts left on the kitchen table, and Bibles beside the bed – where the ash-tray used to be. And the relentless happiness of Sally, shining like the summer sun, had a depressing effect on Dave. He scurried from its light like a badger.

Jack didn't know the full story, but he could tell Dave was as miserable as sin. Only on the rarest of occasions did he go back to the flat, and Lily never appeared again. Ruth did, but, and more often Lockie's old girlfriend, Laura.

"Don't talk to me about singin'," Dave answered when Jack asked why Laura and Lockie had split up. The group at the Buckie Gelder had lost both, Laura because she left, and Lockie because he wasn't wanted by the rest of them without Laura.

Whether or not Laura was the first person that Sally brought to Jesus, only God alone knew. Anyway, the pair of them had started up a gospel singing group – country style – and had even started touring the countryside doing concerts on weeknights. The practising was driving Dave nuts, and the Buckie Gelder was the only place he could get a bit of peace and quiet.

"Ye're a bit hard on her," Jack told Dave about Sally. "It could be a lot worse, ye know."

"Ay, but you don't have to put up wi' it. Bible-thumpin'

from mornin' to night."

The last straw came when Dave opened his lunch-box in the van. They were on a big run to Blackfort Town to drop off a second-hand games machine. There, on top of his piece in the tupperware box, was a tract. He nearly went ape.

"Luk …! I ask ye, luk …" He was just about speechless, shaking the wee bit of paper in Jack's face.

"She's only jokin', so she is," said Jack. "Sure it says, 'Man shall not live by bread alone,' doesn't it? She must have put in a chocolate biscuit an' all."

"She's niver jokin', that's the trouble," Dave said through his teeth. He made up his mind there and then. That was it. He wasn't going to be made a laughing-stock of any more.

When Jack arrived that night at the Buckie Gelder, Dave was already there at the bar. He was by himself and had his suitcase packed and at his feet.

"Where are you off til?" Jack feared the worst, and was right.

"A don't know. Anywhere. I'll mebbe just sleep in the van thenight, an' work that one out in the mornin'."

Only concerned up to a point, and not at all surprised, Jack wondered about his job.

"Ye want me to come down here, just, in the mornin', like?"

"Oh, ay," Dave said. "What d'ye want to drink?"

Jack was fairly relieved about the job situation.

"And Sally? How's she takin' it?"

"I dunno. She wasn't in. But there won't be so much sunshine and joy about the place now – eh?"

The night hadn't really got going at the Buckie Gelder. It was still half empty when a swollen-faced Sally came through the door. Laura was at her side, eyes flashing, with a "last-chance-saloon" sort of look about her. Timidly, as if entering into hell itself, followed Ruth. She looked all round her, as if demons were likely to be behind every chair and under every stool. Sally went straight up to Dave, and stood with one hand on her hip and the other on the bar. There was a bit of the old look about her. Dave was edgy. He half expected to get his drink poured over him. If only.

"So what are ye runnin' away from now?" she said after a pause to get her breath.

"I'm not runnin' away from nathin'. If ye want me back ye'll have to stap all this oul religious nonsense."

"Are you askin' me to choose between you and the Lord?" Sally asked, her eyes filling up like two of the vodka optics behind the bar.

Dave just looked at her. She wasn't the person he married. He didn't know her any more. And he certainly didn't like her any more either.

"Well?" she said. Dave still said nothing, but looked round at Jack for support. Nobody else was going to get involved. It was hard to look as if you weren't listening.

"Right, Dave, A'm sorry, but A've no choice. I'm sticking with the Saviour."

Dave was completely thrown. Sally was dumping him, even though it was him had left her. And in front of his friends in the bar? The humiliation was devastating. And she had said his name so softly as she turned and walked out. There was no huff about it.

There wasn't much banter from Dave that night. The others tried to cheer him up, but they had enough sense not to banter him about it too. Where Dave went to that night was anybody's guess. He had gone quiet and wasn't drinking, so he could have taken the van.

In the morning, when Jack arrived, the van was there at the back of the Buckie Gelder, but no sign of Dave.

He waited, and waited, and then decided he would go and try at the flat. Sally answered the door. She had more than the artificial smile he had got used to seeing. It was like somebody fit to burst with childish joy.

"Come in, come in, Jack," she said.

Dave was there, in body and in spirit, great spidery legs and all. Not much of a catch for Sally or God, but a big loss to the Buckie Gelder and Jack.

Just as Reg had finally got into the police, his wife left him.

And as sure as Dave and Sally were back in business as a couple, so Dave was bound to lose his "job."

Jack trudged back up home across the Green. He could see it all in front of him – nothing. He knew for sure Dave wouldn't backslide. No chance of that with Sally at his back. In a month's time Dave would have his own van, and be driving kids around to gospel meetings, and up and down the country. The only goods he would touch now would be good-living. And not so much as a "What'll you do now, Jack?" from either of them. At least, not as far as his contribution to the black economy was concerned.

"There's no work theday. Dave's off," he explained to his mother when he got back inside the house. Ten minutes was as long as he could sit there. Talk about being bored. Just going out for a walk would be better.

"A thought you cud drive now?" his mother asked.

"Ay, but A haven't ma licence yet." After a few more minutes fidgeting and footering about, he put his jerkin back on.

"A'm away out to the phone to see if Reg is in."

Reg didn't work regular hours. As a cadet with the Police Department, he had night classes, and a lot of his duty-training time in the Barracks was in the evenings. So mornings might be okay.

Yes. At last something was going Jack's way. Reg was in,

and at a loose end too – "I'll drop down an' pick ye up. Where are ye?"

The passenger seat in Reg's car was the height of luxury compared with that of Bugsy's van. On the road back to Reg's chalet bungalow, they caught up with each other's news. Neither had been back to the band since it became the James M'Carroll Memorial, though Reg still kept in touch with most of them.

"I wouldn't be allowed out wi' them, not now I'm in the police."

"Sure you never paraded anyway – ye always walked wi' the Guild, so ye did."

"Ay I know, but ye see, now I'm in the police I wouldn't be allowed out wi' the Guilds either."

There was some weakness in Reg's chain of logic, but Jack wasn't much interested in either now.

"A'm in the NIPD band now, ye know, but it's a military band. It's not the same."

Jack knew what he meant. "Military" bands had brass instruments, of course, but then they had reed ones as well – saxophones, clarinets and the like. You could never get them tuned together in cold weather. They were desperate squeaky.

Reg's house was a sad case of decaying suburban grandeur. Since Jane had left him, it had accumulated a bachelor-pad veneer, but it was still a wife-furnished semi. The decor could be spruced up again if necessary, but even Jack noticed everything was grubby. Where in heaven's name would you find a house that had a woman's touch underneath, and a row of unwashed, mostly empty, milk bottles along the living-room mantelpiece? Only a woman could make a house Protestant-looking, for a man certainly couldn't.

"D'ye ever see Jane?" Reg gave Jack a sharp look at the mention of his ex and sat down before answering.

"Na."

That was the end of that conversation. Jane had been doing a line with a policeman for years, and it was her that encouraged Reg to join. He did see the other party sometimes at work, but until they got their divorce it was all a bit awkward.

"Any chance o' helpin' me to get my driving licence?" Jack had this one objective. It was his ticket to a proper job.

"Did yer man Beggs not learn ye when ye were workin' to him?"

"Ay, but not wi' L-plates or nothin'."

"An' what if we were stapped?" Reg said. "I would lose ma job."

There was a long pause in the crack till Jack thought about what he was going to do.

"Did ye ever think of joinin' the police?" Reg asked, with a look of potential excitement under his raised eyebrows.

"The peelers? Na." The changed look on Reg's face told him not to add, "… catch yerself on."

"But the money's good, overtime, an' … the' would get ye yer licence. Ye can go for drivin', the ban', community work, anythin' at all that turns ye on."

"I thought ye could end up fightin' terrorists?"

"Not if ye don't want to."

Jack was definitely interested, even excited now that he was seriously thinking about it.

"An' I could learn to drive a Land-Rover?"

Reg said he would get him the forms. And he was back at the M'Cleans' that night with them. There was an entrance exam, but. It had taken Reg ages to pass it, and he was by no means stupid. It turned out that the problem wasn't the exam, but the aptitude tests. He hadn't the right attitude – something to do with his suspicion that Jane was seeing a policeman, but he still couldn't put his finger on it. He finally passed whenever Jane left him.

It was a wee dawdle for Jack. In less than five weeks after he sent in the forms, he was actually there – living as a fresher cadet, in a dorm, in the Police Academy. You could hardly credit it. Trainee Constable John M'Clean. Nobody was prouder in the whole Newbiggins estate than his mother and John M'Clean, Senior.

Jack was trying on his new uniform, cap under his arm, and then on his head, and then back under his arm. The locker beside his bed was just like army ones you see in the war pictures. It was hard to get a full view of himself in the wee mirror he had propped up at an angle against his pillow.

"The weemen'll be fechtin ower ye."

A country voice came from a round, red-faced occupant of the next bed. Addie Johnstone was lying back reading *The Police Cadet's Guide to Traffic Control.* He put it down and sat up.

"Ye for hittin' the toun thenicht then?"

"No, I've got a class over at the university – on youth work, or psychology or something."

"A wouldnae bother wae that ava. Ye'll end up motorin weans roon in a mini-bus. See deprived children? Waur nor terrorists, they are. In fact, that's exactly what they are."

"Where is it you come from agane? Blackfort?"

"Ay, jist ootside. Ye merried?"

"No. I was goin' out wi' a girl from the Blackfort Road, ye know, here in Bigganreek, but nothin' steady now."

"Stay oot o' the Special Branch if ye'r frae the Claw, for the mair ye're in the polis o' yer ain free will, the'll no gie ye thair fu trust."

"What classes is it you're doin' then?" Jack wasn't used with country folks, especially ones his own age.

"Motor-bikes, motor-bikes and mair motor-bikes. A hae a yin-track mind."

"A suppose you'll be doin' the language classes too?" Jack thought Addie would have a head start with the Ulster-Scots ones anyway.

"Ye maun dae them, for they're compulsory."

"Huh! Not that Ulster-Scotch is gonna be much use on a motorbike, though."

Addie looked at Jack to see if he was taking the hand out of him. "Ye're richt eneuch there," he said.

"Where's this ye're for thenicht?" Addie asked, lifting his *Guide* again.

"The college."

"Oh ay. Ye dinnae wear yer uniform tae clesses, ye know."

"Ay, A know." Jack put his cap back in the locker, and started to get changed.

There were classes in sociology, riot control, traffic law, special skills, vehicle maintenance, language and local culture, criminal law, police history – all sorts. Some were in the Academy, some were up at the University, and some were run here and there by teachers from the civil service. That part was a bit like going back to school. But then school wasn't anything like that at all. The best part was out of the Academy doing the real thing in among real policemen. He never thought of police as having a sense of humour, but the crack and banter was nonstop. Except when the top officers were about.

By the summer, Jack was out with Addie Johnstone on police motor-bikes. Even though he was still a cadet, when you had all that gear on you, nobody would have thought it. He could see why that was what Addie liked best. When he saw people outside that he recognised, they had no idea who he was.

The Ulster-Scots class was run by Miss Young from the Ministry of Culture. Jack thought it wise to tag along with Addie.

"Fair faa yis, yin an aa," said Miss Young to the class, and pointed to the response chalked up on the blackboard as they were settling in.

"Fair faa ye, Miss Young."

"Ye neednae caa me Miss Young. Jist caa me Nosa. A'm the Dominie fur tha neist twa-thie nichts."

Addie whispered in Jack's ear, "She's no sae young, richt eneuch."

"Mair lown!" she said severely. "Houl yer wheesht, you. Quhit dae the caa ye?" She was looking straight at Addie, who stood up to answer.

"Addie Johnstone, Miss."

Taken by Addie's respectful discipline, she smiled.

"Ye'r no gart stan tae attention ilka time A speir at ye, Addie. Ye maun be yin o tha lairners frae tha Polis?"

"Yes, Miss."

"Ay, Nosa," she corrected him. "Weel. Cud onieboadie gie iz quhit ye micht crie tha NIPD gin ye wur taakin Scotch?"

"Blek besterts," somebody called out from the back. There was an uneasy silence, but when Addie and Jack laughed, they all did.

"Yea, yea," said Miss Young. "We hae the same auld jokes ilka yeir – 'Black B's', 'the ORR-U-See', 'the Or'nge Peelers'."

"A niver heerd thon last yin afore," Addie whispered, not understanding how an orange could be peeled by anything other than a thumb.

"Addie!" said Miss Young again, slapping her hand on the back of the textbook she was holding closed. "Apen yer buiks at Chaiptèr Seiven, noo, an owerset tha furst twa pages intil Inglis. Aaboadie."

"Fun? Eh, what?" Jack muttered to Addie. "She would make sex seem like hard goin', so she would."

Addie looked up at her and smirked. "Richt eneuch."

July, and the Guild's Fair Day in Bigganreek. There were no classes for a fortnight – the whole of the Guild's "Week" – for every single policeman was needed for traffic and crowd control. Addie and Jack were out on their own for the first time, on their bikes, at the bottom of the Blackfort Road, just coming into the city centre. When the parade was approaching, a message came through the radio on Addie's bike. He had to stop the traffic coming onto the road at the Avon Street junction. They had already turned the traffic lights off and were directing the traffic by hand until the first of the parade came in sight. The booming drums and flapping colours of the distant banners seemed strange, far off.

Addie stopped the flow of traffic from Avon Street for the last time, and Jack went down to the other end of the block of shops to stand by their motor bikes. It would be easy for Jack to see his old Fleshers Guild banner coming. And his old band. And nobody would know him with his helmet on. Little did he think a year ago, coming down that road himself, that he would be standing here in full uniform today.

At the sound of the bands, people were gathering at the edge of the footpath, coming out of side-streets and cantering past to get to a better vantage point. Jack could hear footsteps coming up the alley behind him from the back of the shops. Before he turned he heard, "Feng! – Feng, Feng!" three thudding cracks. At least one hit him on the shoulder and spun him round and down. Before he had even worked out what had happened, Addie was at him in a flash, helmet off and making him comfortable.

"Houl on Jack. Ye'll be aa richt. The ambulance is on its way."

Jack could feel a warm sticky patch on his left side. It only hurt if he tried to move.

"Get back, an' gie him a bit o' air," Addie said to the crowd that had gathered round, mostly women out to see their menfolk. "Any nurses or a doctor?"

One woman came forward and knelt down. She undid the zip and the buttons down the front of his jacket, carefully, one by one. Then she lifted one side up slowly and looked inside. She put her scarf tightly against his side, inside the jacket. That hurt all right. "Could ye hold that tight?" she said to Addie.

"All right, son," she said, looking closely into his eyes. "What's your name?"

"Jack … Jack M'Clean."

She could hardly hear him. "Jack?" He gave a wee nod. "Is it sore to talk?" He gave another. The woman looked a bit like Alice Agnew, Ruth's mother, but it wasn't.

The crowd gathered around him had got bigger and bigger. There were bandsmen and Guildsmen with white gloves. Some of the young bucks were f'ing and blinding about the gunman.

"There's no call for that language," said one Guildmaster with a particularly fancy cape over his regalia. It was as if their swearing was the biggest sin that had been committed so far that day.

"It's Jack M'Clean," he heard somebody say in the crowd. "John M'Clean's wee lad from Champion Street." The cursing and swearing got worse and worse as the news spread back along the halted parade.

"Keep yerself awake, Jack." He opened his eyes again; there were faces there he recognised.

Sammy Agnew, Ruth's dad, came pushing through with deacon pole, white gloves and an impressive rustling of Total Abstinence Guild regalia. "Jack," he said, putting his white-gloved hand behind Jack's head, and his other on his red-stained chest. "Jack, are you all right?" It was hard to stay awake. He opened his eyes again. His mother and auntie Betty were behind Sammy, waiting with their arms round each other.

"Jack, do you hear me?" Sammy went closer to his face. Jack could smell the meths. He'd forgotten that Sammy's shining baby-face was the result of using meths as an after-shave. It gave him a funny smell for a Total Abstainer.

"Jack, are you saved? Born agane? Ye've got to do it, right now." Jack tried to speak, but he couldn't. He opened his mouth and moved his lips. Sammy smiled reassuringly, a long warm smile, and patted him on the head as he stood up. When Jack opened his eyes again it was his mother. She was wearing a coat and a brooch he hadn't seen before. It was warm and wet, lying here, just like soaking in the bath. … He loved sleeping in the bath.

Chapter 12

Caught Red-Handed

It takes a long time to recover from a single close-range bullet wound to the lower shoulder, even if you are lucky enough for it not to hit any vital organs. In Jack's case there were complications, for two bullets had hit him and only one of them where it wasn't considered mortal.

The first familiar face he saw when the sulphur-smoke shired in the front of his eyes was Lily, standing at the bottom of the hospital bed, with Ruth. When Lily saw that Jack had come round, she burst out in a sob and tried to turn it into a laugh.

"Look, Jack's woke up – get his ma in quick."

Lily went up to the seat beside Jack and took his right hand. His left arm was bandaged across his chest.

"I'm sorry, Jack," she said.

"What for?" It surprised Jack that he could talk without it hurting him. There were all sorts of tubes running into him. Maybe he was drugged up to the eyeballs. Lily was fantastic looking. He didn't remember seeing her so unbelievably pretty before.

"A've brung ye a wee card an' some black grapes, an' some sweets. D'ye want me to get ye somethin' to read?"

"How long am A in here?" Jack asked. Lily's eyes filled and she said nothing. He looked over at the cards and things on the side. "A thought red an' white flowers was unlucky," he said.

"Don't tell your ma that. They're from her."

"It was her toul me they were unlucky," he said, just as Ruth and his mother arrived.

"Thon's just an oul superstition," said Ruth, as Jack's mother took Lily's seat. He half expected her to start blubbing all over him, but she was calm, as if a long, long worry was over, but she didn't want to believe it.

"Am A goin' to be able to stay on in the police?"

"That's the least o' yer worries, son. But ye can ask them yerself when the' come in agane."

It took Jack some time to get used to this coming and going. He drifted off and when he opened his eyes again they were gone.

"Nurse, was there visitors in to see me there?"

"Yes, John. Your mother and your girlfriend and another girl I think."

"My girlfriend? Did she tell you that?"

"I just know these things. But ye get tired with too much excitement."

"Is there anything to read? Ye know, till Lily gets me somethin'?"

"I'll get you a magazine. There's always the Gideon Bible there. It wouldn't do ye any harm."

"Just the job, seein A'm one o' Gideon's Chosen Few." The nurse gave him a strange look, not understanding what he was getting at.

"Are they treating you all right?" It was a high-ranking Police Officer, looking remarkably human at the bedside.

"The nurses here are great, brilliant, sir."

"Good."

"Will I be allowed back on duty, sir? I mean, to finish at the Academy?"

"I'll make sure of it myself. But I don't think you'll be on a motor-bike again."

Only folk from the Claw came to see him: nobody at all from Newbiggins apart from his mother and father. Or so he thought. Sally had been three times, once with Dave and twice by herself. But Jack was out cold each time. It was almost as if he only woke up for certain visitors. And they just came and went at all times – or so it seemed. But then Jack had lost all sense of time in the hospital. For weeks he wasn't sure whether it was night or day as he slipped in and out of sleep. People just appeared at the bedside. The sooner he was able to get home and choose who to see the better.

Sammy Agnew came by himself. "I told you, Jack. Safe in the arms of the Saviour." Jack said nothing. For an instant, he was too weak to speak.

"The doctor says you'll be out soon, but you'll not be able to climb any stairs. Do you have any friends in the country you could stay with? If you're stuck, Alice, an' Ruth an' me could put ye up in our back room."

Jack nearly forgot himself in his haste to say "no thanks." It was strange that the wee two-up, two-downs in the Claw had a back scullery you could use as a bedroom, while the bigger, new houses on the estates had only a living room and a big kitchen on the ground floor.

"Ye'll be home before ye know it anyhow," Sammy smiled.

Whatever the reason, Jack was taen til the back scullery o his auntie Betty's in Fiji Street. Sammy called and said that he needed to go to the country for proper peace, and he'd be better off there.

Funny the wee hooses cud take mair folk nor the big new yins. "It maun be the size o' the rooms," he thocht. It was like being a wean again, like the time he broke his leg at the fitbaa. He even took a notion to see his old Annuals again, and his ma had, believe it or no, kept ilka yin. But he could get up and doiter in and oot the kitchen parlour, and even sit on a sate at the front door on a guid day. It was like being an oul-timer noo.

Grannie Beggs didnae come in tae Betty's, and as far as Jack could tell, Betty never seemed to bother with her any more. For certes, there was nae sign o Dave or Sally or onie o the Beggses. He had forgotten that grannie Beggs was dead.

The folk that maist frequented auntie Betty's noo was the Gambles. No just Lily, but Kenny and Billy, and even Ernie – wha offered tae mak Jack a wheen o gadgets tae apen things wae the yin hand.

Lily did that much aboot auntie Betty's hoose, it was getting like the way it micht'a been if they had got married and taen Eric Bates's auld hoose. The odd morning Jack even woke up tae his double favourite – Lily, and scrambled eggs on toasted heel o plain loaf.

"Wud ye get that thing out o' my house." Betty couldn't stand Ernie's pigeons.

"A just brought it round to say hello to Jack," he said. "It'll not do any harm."

"Well, this isn't a zoo, an' I can't stan' birds."

"What's that, then?" Ernie said, nodding to the budgie cage in the corner. "A tortoise?"

"Pigeons is dirty, and I have an invalid in the house."

Ernie just ignored Betty, and took his prize pigeon ower tae the cage to say hello to Peter, the pale green budgie. "See Peter," Ernie said into the ear of his jumpy pigeon, "he's been learnt to talk and now he's part o' the family." He turned to

Betty. "A think Peter could even feed the cat one o' these days."

If Jack didnae watch it, he would lose the incentive tae get better. Life was cosy there, waited on hand an foot, an only seein the folk he wanted to see.

"D'ye no reckon ye hae bin loafin' roon the hoose lang eneuch?" Addie had just turned up oot o the blue. "The lads in the Barracks haes a desk fixed up for ye on the grun flair. Nae stairs ava, an ocht ye hae need o, we'll dae it oorsels."

"A'd love tae get back, Addie. But the doctor says A have to get a signin' off line, an' he won't write it till A'm fit for the stress as well as the graft. Ma nerves is away to hell."

"Ye'll no be gettin onie better stuck here in the Claw, wi' riots near every nicht, wull ye?"

"A niver hear a thing. Sure it's completely dead roun' here."

"Ye hae need o' a full break – like the evacuees durin' the war. Hae ye onie freens in the country?"

"Na. Ye mean like, way out there where you come from? Na. My mother's folks is all supposed to have come from Drumcrun, near Blackfort, but that was in her great-grannie's day. The' had a wee shop in Northdyke Street. But there's no connection now, A don't think. Anyway, me an Lily's thinkin' o' gettin' married soon."

"What did the' caa yer ma's folks – the yins at cum frae Drumcrun?"

"Hyndman. No, that was my ma's name. Madole, A think."

"Niver. That's ma ain mither's name. Did ye ever hear tell o' the Twa Touns at Drumcrun?"

Jack hadnae heerd yin word o sic places, the mair it micht'a bin the very airts his ain folk hailed frae, generations back. Whiles, he had gien it some thocht at the leid classes in the Academy, for there was a load o that sort o thing skailed aboot then – roots and sic-like.

He turnt Addie's offer o a holiday at his folks' ower in his heid, but there was nae chance o him lea'ing Lily ahint for onie mair nor a day or twa.

"A tell ye what, A wudn't mind a run down some day, but, just tae see what way your half lives."

It was Jack's first run oot in a motor frae the shooting. The baith o them talked o aa sorts on the road, but Jack was that wabbit that, whiles, he would drap off.

"A thought it was Blackfort ye lived in," quo he as they passed through the toun and on tae Ballypeden.

"Na, it's on oot this road. A'll show ye whaur A leeve. It's aboot the same far as we've come."

Addie pointed oot a twa-storey hoose on the roadside after twa-three mile. They driv straucht by it. "A'm takin ye tae yer auld ancestral hame, oh ye venerable Madole." They lauched.

"What the heck?" Jack speired, but wae his interest weel riz.

Jessie Madole's hoose was the exact thing Jack thocht an ancestral hamesteading should be – apen fire, the lot. Maist folksy o aa was Jessie Madole hersel, sut in the ingle happed up wae dizzens o crochet shawls an sic. She taen a muckle interest in Jack, preeing ilka thing aboot his family.

"He's mendin frae gettin hut wae twa bullets alow the oxter, Miss Madole," sayed Addie, but auld Jessie wasnae the least interestit in his condition jist noo.

"It's gye dangerous leevin in the city," quo she, "an gye wickit forbye. Ye wurnae mixed up wae ocht, wur ye?"

"Na," Addie gien repone for Jack. "He's in the polis. He was guardin a parade."

"Oh ay?" Jessie wasnae impressed. "Sae you'd be yin o Matt Madole's yins. He tuk a wee fancy-guids shap in the citie. They used tae leeve here ye ken. A couldnae say quhit they left for; it maun hae bin for siller. Quhit dae ye say, sinn? Quhit wud ye want tae leeve in Bigganreek for?"

Jack gien nae repone. He wasnae expectit tae. Auld photos were brocht oot. Yin had a cart-horse athoot a cart, and a weefella on its back. "Thon's Matt Madole," Jessie sayed. "Thon's yer great granda. He thocht he was a cowboy. Weel, he wud'a bin, gin he hadnae up an flittit tae Bigganreek."

"There's ithers o oor ain fowk flittit tae Americae, is that no richt, Miss Madole? Quhit aboot aa thae letters?"

"Och them. Uncle Tam? Quo he – 'yis're mair stoot-hairtit nor me' – just acause we pit the minnyster oot o the meetin hoose yin Sabbath. An him's the boy that flittit til Americae. He writ that, richt eneuch – 'yis're mair stoot-hairtit nor me.' Quhit dae ye think o that, sinn?"

Jessie Madole had her tay brocht tae her, and Jack, Addie, Tam an the rest o the hoose sat roon a muckle table. There were plates and plates o aa soarts o breid. "Tam, you butter quhitiver breid Jack wants," Jessie cried frae the fireside. She maun hae taen tent o Jack's airm in a sling after all.

Ither folk cum ben the hoose efter tay was done. And it was back tae Jessie in the ingle. The inquisition stairtit up agane. "A jalouse yis dinnae gan tae Meetin, in the city? Yis'd be ower big gat for that?"

"Na," Jack sayed. "Jist wi' the Guilds an that."

"An A jalouse ye dinnae believe in Gude?"

"Oh? Well, … Ay, …" The gaithered nebby neighbours, and kin, were watching intently. Ilka ee was on him.

"Are ye feerd tae talk o Jesus as yer freen?"

"Feerd? Me? Na."

"Ye know richtly quhit A mean. Are ye saved?"

Wae sic a jury there was a straucht answer required.

"Well … but not very long." Silent stares. "A mean, yes."

Jack imagined he could see a smile on Sammy Agnew's face. This new sense o belonging gien him a wairm glow in his hairt. He couldnae'a felt mair at hame gin he had'a been back at the Claw.

The first day back at work was like another holiday, with the same amount of fuss. Jack had a "blue card," the disabled workers certificate. The rest of the lads were going to organise a stag party for Jack to coincide with his 21st birthday.

"Ye fit to lift a drink, Jack?"

He couldn't raise his left arm above waist height, and that was permanent.

The "back-to-work" interview was with the desk sergeant in the Barracks, rather than his tutor at the Police Academy. The medical report certified, clause by clause, what physical tasks he would be able to perform, and what he couldn't. But the psychological report was more of a cause for concern.

"You have to avoid all stress, Jack," Sergeant Keith Naylor explained. "Do you feel up to outside assignments?"

"What sort of things?"

"Well, I'm putting a team together on a fraud investigation at Wrights Lifts. But there may be paramilitary involvement. Would that worry you?"

"Not at all. Why would it?"

"What about community policing down the city centre? I know there's no community down there, but it's the only place we can go on foot patrol."

"Look, anything at all: I'm not bothered. What about the boys that got me? What's the crack there?"

"That's the last thing you want to get into. We know who did it, but just trust us. We have that under control."

"Who? A mean, give us a break. Ye think I don't want to see them caught?"

"Okay. But it's only intelligence. It's not like they're clever. They're gonna try the same move again, but we're watching this time – and before you say anything, Jack, you're not going to be used in the trap. No way. How would I explain that on your progress report?"

But Jack had to face down his own personal nightmare. Until he went back out on crowd control, and even stood at the same spot, it would be like any phobia.

He wasn't scared. There was no motor-bike uniform; just the ordinary light NIPD one, with shirt and tie. And six of the best experienced peelers you could hope for between him and any possible danger. They really were the best of mates. Jack felt slightly edgy, but totally safe at the same time. He was sure he would get over this test of his rehabilitation on the right side.

The Guild parade seemed to come down the Blackfort Road much quieter this time, because the other lads were joking with him. They made light of everything so as not to let him dwell on what had happened before. But when the bands got right up to them, there was no possibility of any conversation – the drums would have deafened you. The Claw "district" was well back in the parade, but when they came they were all looking straight ahead. Nobody looked at the group of police standing at Brady's Entry.

Then came Sammy Agnew's Total Abstinence Guild, with Sammy holding one of the banner poles. He was making heavy weather of it as the wind caught the banner and the ribbons at the bottom, usually held by wee lads, whipped free and cracked in the air. Obviously there was a shortage of wee lads for the Total Abstinence Guild. Sammy was looking straight ahead too and didn't spot Jack. His white gloves had been stained by the reddy varnish off the banner pole. It crossed Jack's mind that it might be blood, but Sammy was the last person not to have washed his gloves a year on.

And then came Cherryhill Silver Band – as was. Jack moved forward to the edge of the pavement so that the lads in the band couldn't miss him. There they came, but nobody looked in his direction. As the bass drum passed, it was big Tommy, sweating as always. And the new name painted proudly on the drum: "John (Jack) M'Clean Memorial – Bigganreek." That couldn't be right! No! ...

Maybe if he shut his eyes again he would dream of waking up in hospital, or at auntie Betty's or surrounded by friends, somewhere else. It was warm and wet, lying there, just like soaking in the bath ... He loved sleeping in the bath.

"He's rannerin'," Addie said, starting to panic. "If thon ambulance disnae come soon, he'll be a goner."

"It's all right, son," said Sammy Agnew, placing his blood-stained gloved hand on Addie's shoulder, "I think he was just catched in time."

Brady's Entry was right at the bottom of the Blackfort Road, near the city centre. It was a grey, commercial zone, far removed from the old redbrick Claw. A year on from the murder at that very spot, it was virtually deserted. On the day of the next Guild Parade, a single rose lay against the wall corner, at the back of the footpath. In front three women in black coats were huddled together like "three craas on the wall." Despite their arms linked for comfort, each one was as lonesome as ever. Nobody else wanted to watch the parade from that spot, for as each band approached it would stop playing. Only the piercing, echoing tap of a side drum, then, at the spot a cry of "Band, Een Richt!" and the side drummer would tap the wooden rim of his drum, in time with the crunching rhythmic sound of marching feet. The women in black weren't there to see the parade, only to see how their loss was given respect. And they wanted to search the approaching colourful pageant. If they could re-live the last thing that Jack had seen, it might just help them connect. It was mizzling, more of a damp mist than a drizzle. As the bright, bounding river of colour came closer they strained to trace the rainbow through their damp eyes.

Each Chapter on parade had a story to tell in its banner painting. On top of many of the banners, black ribbons had been tied. They were strips of about two or three inches wide of jet black silk, tied in a large fancy bow to the cross pole across the top. From these cross poles the banners were hung, the colours given an extra sparkle because of the contrast with the black rosettes.

From the spot, the black bows on top of the banners came swooping, bobbing down the Blackfort Road like a line of Ravens. They almost looked like they were carrying the banner pictures beneath them. Food for thought, perhaps, to anybody tempted to think of the Claw as only bricks and mortar. Or for those who thought of the people as nothing but flesh and bones. The promise of the rainbow, when the spectators knew how to trace it, might not be in vain.

With the people having left the Claw for the day, the new development had fallen scary silent. Ten hundred nice new houses and maisonettes, with not a single chimney between them. A district heating scheme was taking care of all that now, with a new, centralized service. Towering out of the heating block stood a single, tall aluminium chimney where, almost every day, two enormous crows sat at the top, their feathers fluffed by the warm, smokeless updraught.

But this new Claw seemed like a corpse to the youngest of the three women in black as she walked back from the parade, through its deserted streets. The mews and closes had lost their novelty value with their brown metric brick facades, up and down, in and out, no two the same. Wee gardens had been planted here and there to give a soft edge to the scars left by the scattering of the encampment. Some rehoused survivors were still living there, like Lily herself, or the Kavanaghs and even Hambo Jack. Just like the last stragglers of a mighty demobbed army.

Nobody else was left to redd up this Titanic Age scrap heap. Even before any of them realised that the Claw was being officially stood down as a slum, the reset of its new "civvy" streets had been planned. Urban regeneration yes, but not the Claw born again. Lily sat down in her empty house and cried out loud over everything she had lost. What on earth had happened to it all? After all the "if onlys," she could only hope. The Claw's unending dawn was not composed of bricks and mortar, flesh and bones, or painted silk. Only the other side of the rainbow.

Psalm 78

1   Attend, my people, to my law;
         Thereto give thou an ear;
     The words that from my mouth proceed
         Attentively do hear.
2   My mouth shall speak a parable,
         And sayings dark of old;
3   The same which we have heard and known,
         And us our fathers told.

. . . . .

9   The sons of Ephraim, who nor bows
         Nor other arms did lack;
     When as the day of battle was
         They faintly turned back.
10   They brake God's cov'nant and refus'd
         In his commands to go;
11   His works and wonders they forgot,
         Which he to them did show.

. . . . .

22   For they believ'd not God, nor trust
         In his salvation had;
23   Though clouds above he did command,
         And heav'ns doors open made,
24   And manna rain'd on them, and gave
         Them corn of heav'n to eat.
25   Man angel's food did eat; to them
         He to the full sent meat.

54   Unto his holy border then
         The Lord his people led,
     Ev'n to the mount which his right hand
         For them had purchased.
55   The nations, which in Canaan dwelt,
         By his almighty hand,
     Before his people's face he drove
         Out of their native land.

(Scottish Psalter, 1650)

Psalm LXXVIII

The story o' God's folk an' their hamecomin;
how they thraw'd, an' war dang
wi' God; their wastin an' their walin:
ane o' the grandest sughs o' lang-syne.

1   Hearken, my folk, till my bidden;
     lout yer lugs till the words o' my mouthe:

2   My mouthe I sal rax wi' wyss redin;
     frae lang-syne, I sal tell yo the sugh:

3   What we hae a' hearken'd, an' ken'd o';
     an' our faithers hae tell'd till oursel.

. . . . .

9   Sic-like war the lads o' Ephraim:
     weel dight an' a' wi' their bows,
     they turn'd i' the day o' weir:

10 They bade-na the tryst o' God,
     nor thol'd in his bidden till steer.

11 His doens an' a' they forgat,
     an' his wonners he loot them see.

. . . . .

22 For they lippen'd them nane ontil God;
     nor trysted his ha'din sae heal

23 Tho' the cluds he had tell'd frae abune;
     an' the yetts o' the lift he unsteekit:

24 An' toom'd down atowre them manna till eat;
     an' corn o' the lift till them streekit.

25 Bread o' the brightest ilk carl cou'd pree;
     he airtit their gate the fou o' sic victual.

54 Bot them he gar'd fuhre till his halirude-side;
That height o' his ain, he coft wi' his ain right
han'.
55 An' drave out afore them the folk o' the lan';
an' rightit their haddin by line, an' gar'd dwall
i' the howffs o' the hethen the clans o' Israel's
weans.

(*The Psalms: Frae Hebrew intil Scottis*, 1871)